OF TH
THE
AND
HOUSE

"The book was so exciting. I felt I was there with Lia and Wolfie trying to rescue Aurora. I loved the characters and the magic." Beth, 12

"There was a lot of action, I wanted to keep reading to find out what happened next!" Grant, 12

"I really liked the book. It was a good plot, she was strong and brave and when you read a bit you wanted to read more." Eilidh, 12

"I liked Lia she was kind and caring when she went to find Wolfie and Aurora by herself it was exciting." Lila, 10

"I liked the spells and it was an interesting way to find out about Orkney, I would love to go there on holiday now." Logan, 11

"Lia's story is touching and beautiful. She had depth. It felt like she was actually speaking to me. She felt real." Lucy, 11

"It was a good book to read on holiday. It kept me interested throughout. It shows a good strong girl character. I really liked her." Mhairi, 12

"Lia was funny. I found her believable because she seemed like a normal girl except she had magical powers. I liked Wolfie and I liked that the broomstick was naughty." - Orla, 10

Of The Wind, The Sea, and The House of Strength
By Joan Dewar

2020 Joan Dewar has asserted her right under the Copyright, Designs, and Patent Act 1988 to be identified as the Author of this work.

Text copyright © 2020 Joan Dewar

Design & Illustration © 2020 Jane Cornwell
www.janecornwell.co.uk

A CIP record of this book is available from the British Library.

Paperback ISBN 978-1-913237-08-0

First published in the UK in 2020 by
The Wee Book Company Limited.
www.theweebookcompany.com

Printed and bound by Bell and Bain, Glasgow, who have a policy in place of ensuring they have best environmental procedures and policies in place at every stage of their manufacturing, administration and dispatch. They use the safest most environmentally-friendly raw materials including inks, papers and associated materials for the benefit of the environment as a whole.

OF THE WIND, THE SEA AND THE HOUSE OF STRENGTH

Joan Dewar

The Wee Book Company

I dedicate this book with much love

to my family, Jim, Lisa, Sally & Darren

and my two best boys Alfie and Charlie,

and not forgetting Geordie!

xxxxxx

Joan Dewar

I dedicate this book with much love
to my family; Jan, Lizzi, Sally & Doreen
and my two best boys Alfie and Charlie,
and not forgetting Gemma
xxxxxx
Joan Dean

Before Wolfie and I flew off on the broomstick into the cosmos, I was already aware of how small and vulnerable our planet is, but only when I saw it on the darkest of nights from space, in all its fragility and beauty did I realise that human kind's most urgent task is to take responsibility for our Earth, and cherish and preserve it.

Vanilia Solveig - White Witch

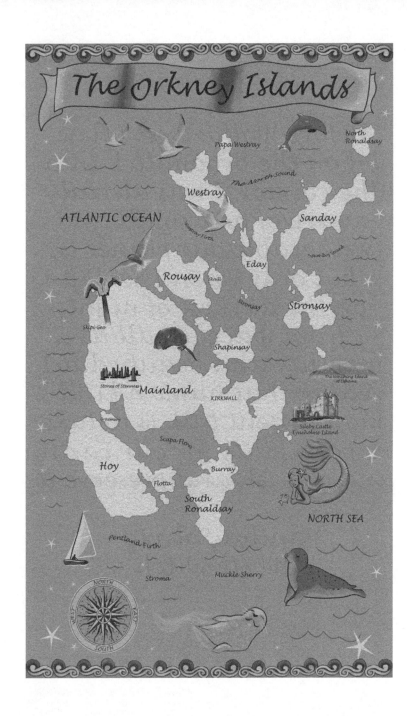

Chapter 1

'Inside or outside deck?' My mum gave me a questioning look.

'Outside,' I answered without hesitation, feeling the need for fresh air. My stomach had started squeezing like a set of bagpipes not long after we had boarded the ferry.

'OK. Good.' She pushed her rucksack under one of the white plastic seats on the outer deck and flopped down, stretching her legs. 'It's a grand day for sitting out.'

'Yeah,' I agreed, plonking myself down on the seat beside her. 'Mum, how long will it be till we get there?'

'We'll arrive in Kirkwall mid-afternoon,' she said, tilting her face up to a hazy winter sun.

'But that's ages,' I groaned.

'Och. It'll pass quickly.' She waved her hand dismissively. 'There's a cinema on the ship. We could watch a film to pass the time, and there's a restaurant. We can get fish and chips later – your favourite.'

Pulling a face, I wrapped my arms around my stomach.

Mum nudged her elbow into my ribs. 'Darlin', you don't need to feel so nervous about the crossing.' She pointed to the sea. 'There's hardly a ripple. Oh look at that.' She pointed out a beautiful rainbow sheen of colours on the smooth surface made by a slick of oil.

The ship's engines vibrated and throbbed into life and, with one braying blast of the horn, we glided smoothly out of Aberdeen's harbour, the ship's motion barely noticeable as we sailed out to sea watching the grey coastline fade to a pale smudge.

'What's up with you?' Mum tapped my knee.

'Jings. I don't know. Wan minute you're jumpy as popcorn on a hot skillet and now there's no gettin' a pleep oot a you.'

My mum was raised on the islands and she hasn't lost her Orcadian way of speaking. She comes out with quirky sayings all the time. I don't remember living in Orkney. I was only a baby when we left, and we've never gone back there – until now.

My stomach made a loud squelching gurgle.

'Of course.' Mum said rummaging through her ruck-sack.' You must be hungry. 'Whar's me specs? You didn't eat any breakfast, did you? Ach. I canna find anything in this muckle bag!' She held her phone directly in front of her nose and narrowed her eyes. 'It's gone ten. You must be starving. Is it too early to eat the picnic?' She delved deep into her rucksack and pulled out two packs of sandwiches. 'Och cheer up, Mrs!' She held them out to me. 'Just be thankful it's a calm day. The North Sea crossing can be gey rough. Here you go. Egg mayo or cheese 'n' pickle?'

'Not hungry,' I mumbled, pulling my knees up and wrapping my arms around them. I hugged them tight, trying to quell my stomach's collywobbles.

Despite the pastel-blue sky and calm sea, I'd foreseen a violent storm coming. I get premonitions, you see. It's not like a gut feeling or a hunch. It's much more. I suppose you could call it my sixth sense. Yeah. I know that makes me sound whacky but it's the truth. You might think having this ability would be awesome but it isn't. All I want is to be just an ordinary, regular kid. I don't want to be different or odd, so I generally keep this weird stuff to myself.

A seagull wheeling in the salty air startled me by dive-bombing us, snatching at the sandwiches Mum was holding out.

'Hey, stop yer thievin', ya cheeky whalp!' she yelled, jumping up and waving her arms in the air to chase the marauding bird away. 'Beuys o beuys. Unbelievable!' She plonked herself down again. 'Here you go. Cheese and pickle or egg mayo? Choose.'

'No, thanks.' I pushed her hand away.

'Uh! Oh… you're no' going to throw up, are you?' She rifled through her bag again.

'Ach, darlin', you've gone the colour of pea soup. Here.' She handed me a plastic bag. 'Use this if you have to.'

'Mum, stop! I'm not going to throw up!'

'Poor lass,' she continued to fuss round me, 'You've never been a good traveller, have you? Why didn't I remember to bring travel sick pills? Try some deep breathing, Vanilia, it'll take your …'

'Mum, I'm fine,' I butted in. Then, abruptly changing the subject, I asked, 'Going to live in Orkney's a new start for us, right?'

'Yeah,' she nodded. 'And?' She raised her eyebrows.

'Well, I've been thinking. When we get there, I don't want to be called Vanilia anymore.'

'Really? Why?' she said, giving me a vague look.

'Mum,' I groaned, 'Vanilia's a crazy name. Nobody

3

gets it. Vanilia sillier two-scoops-Vanilia. The stupid jokes are embarrassing. Why did you give me such a weird name anyway?' I said in a scratchy voice.

'It wasn't me who chose your name; it was your Granny Aurora. She suggested the name, and your father and I liked it. When you meet her, you can ask her about it yourself, but I know it was chosen because of its meaning.'

'What does it mean?' I probed.

She ran her hand through her hair, 'It's from Old Norse. Your first name, Vanilia, means 'Of the wind and the sea', and our surname, Solveig, means 'Of the house of strength.'

Hmmm, I thought, so it was my granny who was responsible for giving me my mad name. She sounded completely random. I couldn't wait to meet her.

'Mum, I just want an ordinary name.'

'OK.' She held up her hands. 'I get it. So, what name would you like to choose?'

'Lia,' I replied firmly. 'I'm going to shorten Vanilia to Lia.'

She leaned back and shoving her hair back from her face said, 'Lia? Aye. I like the sound of it fine, and if it'll make you happy ...' She tilted her head, giving me a long look. 'I'm guessing you're no' very happy right now, are you?'

'You guessed right,' I said, folding my arms. 'Why did we have to move again, Mum? I'm nearly twelve and already I've moved schools four times!'

'Och, Lia, don't let's go over this again.' She gave a weary sigh. 'Awe. Come here. Look. I'm sorry we've had to flit away from your school and your friends again.'

Dropping her arm around my shoulder, she studied me with concerned blue eyes. 'I know fine it's not been

4

easy for you, but you'll make new friends. You're going to have to trust me this move is a good one.' She gave me a forced smile. 'I'm doing this for you.'

'For me?' My mouth fell open. 'Well, you should have asked me first then. Did you even care how I felt about our constantly moving?'

OK, I knew I was behaving like a brat, but I felt really hacked off. I didn't want to have to start all over again. It wasn't that I felt sad about leaving friends behind. The truth is I've never had any real friends. I'm kind of a loner, though not from choice. I've tried making friends, but I don't fit in. Not because of my stupid name, or my mad corkscrew hair. (My mum tries to make me feel better about my red hair by calling it 'Titian' but really it's just plain ginger.) It's not even because of my webbed toes. My guess is other kids sense there's something weird about me. I've learned it's easier to fade into the background and pretend I'm invisible.

Mum held my shoulders and turned me around to face her. 'It's complicated. Look. As soon as we get settled, we'll have that talk. I'll tell you everything about our past, and then I hope you'll properly understand why we have to go back to our roots in Orkney now.'

'But, Mum' – I stood my ground eyeballing her – 'why can't we talk about it now? Mum I need to know .' Her smile faded and her tone turned sharp. 'I've said we'll talk about it when we get settled. I want your grandmother to be with us when we have that conversation. Look. I've promised I'll answer all your questions but' – she raised the flat of her palms to me – 'not right now. OK?'

Her attitude riled me, and this time I wasn't for backing down. 'No, Mum! It's not OK. You owe me an explanation. We've barely got settled somewhere when you decide on a whim to uproot us again. Why do we have to keep moving? And why, just because you've decided on it, do we have to go and live on an island cut-off from everything? Has our going back to Orkney got anything to do with my father's death?' The look on her face told me I was pushing it. My voice faded away.

My father is a mystery. When I think of him it's always as 'Father.' I was very young when he died. I'd never known him, so it doesn't seem natural to call him 'Dad.' I wished Mum would open up to me about him but when I question her about him she just repeats the same old answers.

'Your father died in tragic circumstances. You're too young now to discuss it. I'll tell you more when you're older.'

But I'm old enough now! I thought, desperately wanting to know more, but my mum always made it clear that she wouldn't be drawn on it. As usual I gave up on talk of my father and changed the subject.

'So, what is it going to be like living in Orkney?' Mum scraped a hand through her tangle of blonde hair.

'Well, in lots of ways it'll be a better life than living in a big city. I'm going to use my degree to try to find work in conservation. Did you know that Orkney's at the forefront of the whole country when it comes to renewable energy?'

'Mum,' I sighed, 'you don't need to give me a save the planet lecture. I'm already completely sold on it.'

'I know you are,' she nodded. 'Anyway I think we can make a happy life in Orkney. It's a friendly community. The Orcadians are a kindly folk. They're very tolerant of anyone who might be a wee bit different.' She glanced at me, and I quickly looked away, wondering uneasily if she suspected I felt I was very definitely different from other kids.

'Will we be living close by to Granny Aurora, Mum? Why haven't we kept in touch with her? Why have we never gone back to the islands to see her until now?'

'Och, stop!' My mum gave me her 'discussion over' face.

'Fine,' I said, shaking her arm off and standing up. 'There's no point in talking to you, is there? You never give me answers!'

'Ach,' she said, stretching her hand out to pull me back. 'Don't be like that. Let's not fall out, baby.'

Throwing her the dirtiest look I could muster, I stomped off to explore the lower deck.

Huh. Baby! She calls me a baby. Flippin' heck, I'm nearly twelve! Surely I have a right to know how my father died!

While I fumed and paced the lower deck, going over in my mind all of the times I had failed to get Mum to open up to me about the circumstances that had brought about my father's death, the ship sailed into open sea. A prickle on the back of my neck told me my sixth sense had been right. Black glowering clouds gathering on the horizon turned daylight to an eerie gloom. It started with a whisper, but soon the ship was punching into a northerly gale. First, the sea turned from placid to churning then to

high rolling waves. Everyone out on deck fled to the inner saloons. I felt scared and also guilty about the falling out. I knew my mum always tried to do her best for us, so I retraced my steps meaning to make up with her. I gripped hard on the ship's railings to pull myself along as strong gusts of wind buffeted me back.

When I reached the spiral stairs to the upper deck, a dark shape above cast a shadow over me making me pause and glance up. A sinister-looking black seabird circled above me cawing raucously, as if trying to attract my attention. Squinting up through wet hair that was plastered to my face, I gaped in shock as the bird made a sudden abrupt diving movement before swooping down on me, deliberately beating its wings around my head. My frightened yells got drowned out by the howling wind. Throwing my arms up to protect my face from its stabbing beak I slipped and lost my footing on the rain-soaked deck, hitting my head as I fell. Lying helpless and stunned I recoiled shielding my face with my hands as the bird dipped and hovered menacingly over me. Fixing me with its yellow eye, it snaked its long neck towards me and, shrieking into my face, jabbed at me once more with its razor-sharp beak before flying off into the storm.

Struggling up to my feet feeling dazed, I registered a palpable shift in the atmosphere. The air crackled with energy as silver tongues of forked lightning zigzagged across the sky. That's when it happened. A blinding flash seared into my pupils. A thrumming, buzzing sensation vibrated inside my head. I had the weirdest sense of another version of me looking down on myself, and in this freakish moment a hot prickling feeling flooded my body. In that split second, I felt the two separate versions of me fuse into one. I stood swaying on shaky legs and staggered

9

to the ship's railings, grabbing on to them to steady myself.
Gazing down into flashes of the white-and-grey ocean a
buried knowledge from deep inside me rose and broke free.
I heard myself speak the words:

Peace. Be still.

Instantly, the wind dropped, the sea calmed and the storm
died.
Through a haze of red mist, as if from a great distance I
heard my mother's anxious voice repeating my name.
'Lia! ... Lia!'

Chapter 2

'Where am I?' I let out a muffled groan as I tried to push myself up onto my elbows.

Mum's worried eyes searched mine. 'Oh, dearie-me. You look gey peely-wally. Just lie still and rest.' She tucked a blanket around me. 'You're in the ship's sickbay. They said you can rest here until we dock. Do you remember the storm? You fell and bumped your head?' Stroking my hair, she fretted: 'I think you were briefly knocked unconscious.'

My brain felt too foggy to make much sense of it. 'I think I remember. Yes. I had a scary dream about a huge black seabird attacking me.'

Her face clouded over. 'Shush,' she soothed, smoothing my hair, 'just rest.'

When the ferry finally docked, and our car rolled off, I felt massively relieved to be on dry land again. Did I say 'dry land'? Well, it wasn't that exactly. We headed straight into heavy downpours of rain. I wriggled my bottom trying to get comfortable in the car's back seat, wedged between boxes, bags, rucksacks and a prickly cactus plant.

'Are you sure you feel all right, Lia? Do you think we should head for a doctor just to have you checked out?'

I rubbed the lump on the side of my head. It was

just a bit tender but not really sore. 'I'm OK. Honestly. I'm fine. How far is it until we get there?'

'Och. Not too far now. Here … catch.' Taking a piece of gum from the pack, she tossed it back to me. 'Try chewing. It helps with travel sickness.'

I'd brought a book to pass the journey. A brainteaser. I enjoy doing puzzles and riddles. I'm smart when it comes to solving problems. I like challenging myself.

Sneakily unclicking my seatbelt, I sprawled my legs over a rucksack until I found myself a comfy position, then I opened the book.

'Lia, put the seat belt back on NOW! I know we're on an island, but all the same rules apply!'

'OK! Nippy knickers!' I sat up and strapped myself in again, then picking up the puzzle book I turned to the riddles. 'Mum, here's a riddle for you. Which letter does the ocean remind you of?'

'Easy-peasy,' she answered, pointing at the wide expanse of ocean we were driving alongside. 'It's the C!'

'OK, that was too easy. Here's another one. 'What's …'

She interrupted, 'No more riddles, Lia. My brain's too frazzled to think.'

'Tut! OK. How long till we get there now?' I badgered.

'Wheesht!' She frowned at me in the car mirror, 'Stop your girnin'. That's the second time you've asked me in the last ten minutes.'

'Sorreee!' I said in a singsong voice, 'but I can't wait. I'm excited to see our house.'

'Me too, but Vanilia … oops, sorry … Lia, your keeping pestering won't get us there any sooner. Maybe put the book down – you know reading in the car makes you travelsick.'

I laid the book aside. 'Mum, can I open the window?'

She squinted back at me in the mirror. 'Are you feeling queasy? Yes. Let some fresh air in. Lean out and take deep breaths.' She rolled down the car windows. 'It's not far to go now.'

I sat up and thrust my head out the window gulping in air.

'Yuchhh!' I pulled my head quickly in again. 'Pooo! What's that smell? It stinks.' I gagged.

'It's slurry.' Mum wrinkled her nose. 'Phew, yeah. I'd forgotten the horrible niff here in early spring.'

'What's slurry? Is it as mingin' as it sounds?'

She laughed. 'Aye, it is. It's a mix of cow poo and water. The farmers use it here to fertilise their fields in spring. It helps the crops grow.'

'Disgusting!' I snorted and pulled my jersey top up to cover my nose and mouth as I tried to keep from breathing in the awful pong.

Just as I thought things couldn't get any worse, the sky turned charcoal grey and needles of freezing rain splattered through the open window.

Mum threw her head back and laughed. 'Ach! Dearie me. Typical Orkney weather! Nothing's changed! An umbrella's useless here. It's a riot shield you need!'

'It's not always wet and windy here, is it?' I grumbled.

'Weel, no. Of course, it doesn't always rain here,' she said none too reassuringly. 'We do get sunny lovely days, too, but it can be very blustery in Orkney, especially in the winter months. Have you noticed the lack of trees? They can't survive the winds, see. The weather plays an important part in island life, especially for fishermen and farmers. I'd almost forgotten the many Norse words folks here use to describe the climate. You'll hear folks say things like "it's blowin' up a skolder or a guster or a screever" depending on the wind's strength. My favourite Orcadian word for horrible weather, though, is "ugsome". Our language is a variety of Scottish wi' lots of Norse influence.'

'Hmm.' I grinned. 'It's a great word to describe yucky weather. I like the Norse words. Is that how Granny Aurora speaks? How soon can I meet her?'

Rolling up the window, I noticed my question had annoyed her and spoiled her cheery mood.

'Mum,' I asked tentatively, 'did you and Grannie Aurora fall out?'

She pulled the car over to the side of the road and sat silent for a moment.

When she finally spoke her voice was snappier than usual. 'Lia. I can't concentrate on driving when you keep asking me all those questions!'

'Sorry.' I knew I'd touched a nerve.

'No, I'm sorry, pet,' she said in a weary tone. 'I didn't mean to be cross with you. I'm just tired. Pals?' She gave a small pleading look. 'Come on. Ask me another riddle?'

'Yeah.' I grinned. 'Pals. OK, got one for you. What

room would a ghost avoid?'

'Uh .. uh. I don't know.' She shook her head.

'Do you give up?'

'Aye. I give up.'

'Duhhh. The 'living room, dopey!'

With a chuckle she pulled out into the road again, her cheerful mood restored. She turned the car radio off and began singing in her lilting voice. She often sang. It was in her DNA, I guess, and this lament was one I'd heard her sing many times – a sad song about a maiden who had lost her love to the sea:

In one of those lone Orkney Isles,
There dwelled a maiden fair.
Her cheeks were red, her eyes were blue,
She had golden russet hair ...

She always sang the song with such feeling that I wondered whether it reminded her of my dead father and of happier times.

The view from the car window mesmerised me: we passed by verges ablaze with colourful wildflowers, flat, gentle farmland and, beyond, the towering red jagged cliffs of the coastline. Although I couldn't remember my life here, I felt a strong connection to this remote, wild island swept by wind and rain. After living in the heart of a busy bustling city, I knew that life here was going to be very different. We drove on beneath a sky dulled by grey cloud. The coastal roads hugged long expanses of deserted white sandy bays shelving a silver-sheened ocean. The steady rhythm of the waves lapping the shoreline soothed and lulled me. Something inside me loosened a notch.

'It's lovely hearing the sound of the sea, isn't it,

Mum?' I murmured.

'Ah, can you feel it, too?' She let out a long breath.

'Mmm? Feel what?' I asked, feeling drowsy.

She spoke in a hushed tone. 'Can you feel this island's enchantment? It fairly brims over with ancient lore and traditions. Did you know, Lia, it's said the seven Orkney islands were created from the teeth of a monster?'

'Is that from the folklore stories you told me when I was little?'

'Ah, you remember them! Well, here on these islands it's possible to go to the place where a mermaid once tempted a young man to go with her to her city under the sea. Her eyes took on a faraway look. 'These islands are magical. They'll cast their spell on you, Lia.'

Her voice trailed off as we rounded a gently curving bend. Parking the car on the edge of a wide shingle beach, she exhaled a long slow breath and dropping her head she hugged the steering wheel.

'Beuy. We've arrived.'

Chapter 3

We shouldered our rucksacks and negotiated a winding
path through clumps of long, coarse seagrass. The sandy
track, strewn with delicate pink pearlescent seashells,
led us down to a solitary cottage fronting a crescent-
shaped bay. I'll admit my heart sank a little when I saw
its neglected appearance. It had once been white but had
weathered to an unpleasant greenish-grey. Its ramshackle
outhouse looked as though one good puff of wind would
blow it over, and its mossy tiled roof had a chimney stack
which stuck out at such a wild angle it made the house
look as though it was wearing a crazy party hat. It stood
in a patch of wild, untamed land flanked by wind-bent
cedars bowed down to the sea. I wondered aloud while
approaching the house why a number three had been
daubed on its front door when as far as I could see its only
near neighbour was a lighthouse sited on the headland.

'I expect there'll be many puzzles and mysteries for
you to solve on these islands, Lia.'

'What do you mean?' I said, mystified. 'Awe, Mum,
stop teasing! You're freaking me out!'

As we crunched up the cottage's gravel path, the
sun unexpectedly broke through the clouds creating a
dazzling arc of colour. An amazing double rainbow took
shape in the sky arching directly above us, giving the house

the appearance of an enchanted cottage from a fairy story.

'Bifrost,' Mum whispered.

'What does that mean?' I asked, catching her sense of wonderment.

Gazing up into the heavens, she murmured, 'It's a Norse legend. The Vikings called a rainbow "Bifrost". They believed a rainbow was a flaming bridge which linked the realm of the gods to that of mortals.

Intrigued, I asked, 'What else did the legend say?'

'It was said that, if you saw a rainbow, it meant the gods were paying a visit. The rainbow was believed to be the home of beautiful female spirits called Keeries who were sent to watch over the fate of those below.'

'Oooh! You're giving me goosebumps,' I said, rubbing my arms.

Putting her arms around my shoulders, Mum gave me a tight hug and murmured into my hair. 'This is a special place, Lia. We've been honoured here today.'

The rainbow streaked the evening sky in spectacular hues of red, gold, green, indigo, and violet giving the late afternoon a strange twixt-dark-and-light quality. Mum released me and pointed out a little seaside town a short way along the coast whose spires, harbour and cluster of grey stone houses were visible in the distance.

'That's where your Granny Aurora lives, Lia.'

I felt a tingle of excitement tinged with nervousness. 'Tell me about her, Mum. What's she like? I don't remember her at all.'

'Well, that's no' surprising,' she replied. 'After all, you were only a peedie bairn when we left.'

'So, when can we go to visit her, Mum?'

'Let's just get settled in, then we'll see,' she said, twisting her finger around an unruly curl that had fallen

over her eye.' Mum always does that when she's nervous.
Dumping her heavy rucksack on the doorstep she muttered
to herself, 'Ach. Whar's the key been left?' She searched
around the front step, looking under flowerpots before
finally lifting the coir doormat. 'Aye, here it is. Found it.'

Looking back over my shoulder at the little seaside
town set me wondering again about Granny Aurora. 'Why
haven't you come back to see Granny until now?' I asked.
'What happened between you two back then?'

'Lia,' – she held the key poised – 'could we leave
this conversation until tomorrow? Let's just get in and
settled, eh?'

'OK.' I heard the tiredness in her voice and backed
down. 'We'll save it till tomorrow.'

She turned the key in the lock, repeating in a
weary voice, 'You and I will sit down and talk this through
tomorrow morning. I promise.' I caught a look of sadness
in her eyes. 'It's time you knew everything.' She gave a
small sigh.

When we stepped through the small musty porch
into the cottage I wrinkled my nose. It smelled damp and
unlived in. We explored its cold rooms feeling a bit like
trespassers. I could tell from her face that Mum was having
second thoughts.

'What do you think of the house, Mum?'

'Oh, come here.' She held her arms out to me. 'I
badly need a hug.' Blinking rapidly, she pulled me towards
her, wrapping her arms around me and sticking her nose in
my hair.

'It'll be OK,' I said, patting her back. 'We're both
tired. This will all look better in the morning.'

One glance around the dust-laden sitting room was
enough to confirm there was no clean place to sit down.

She slapped her hand down on the back of a grimy seat raising a cloud of dust.

'Yeuch, look at this stoor!'

All the same, she let herself sink into a battered old armchair. 'This chair looks only fit for the dump. Gosh, that was such a stressful journey. I'm absolutely puggled.' She sounded close to tears.

At the risk of raising more dust I plonked myself down on the sagging sofa opposite. I attempted to sound optimistic: 'Mum, we can fix this place up to be really nice! We have to think positive!' (If I'm honest, I didn't feel it.)

'Aye, you're right!' she said in a steadier voice. 'Sorry, darlin.' She rubbed the back of her neck. 'I'm just tired.'

She turned to face the small window beside her, drawing back its yellowed net curtain. 'We'll get ourselves properly settled in as soon as the furniture arrives. Once this place is cleaned up, it'll be great.' She rubbed her parka cuff on the grimy window pane and in a more positive voice said, 'Come over here, Li. Look.' I went to sit on the arm of her chair and she hooked her arm around my waist, cuddling me into her. 'We're so blessed to have this.'

We both gazed up into a deep-blue velvet sky, scattered with a galaxy of stars.

'My oh my,' she breathed, 'have you ever seen anything quite so bonnie? Look at that. Here, far away from street lights in big cities it makes it possible to pick out the Milky Way from horizon to horizon.' Bright clusters of stars shone down on us as we gazed up into the deep foreverness of space.

Wow! I've never seen a sky as beautiful. I gazed up

at the twinkling stars feeling optimistic. One of the good things about moving up here would be that I get to look out on this amazing sky instead of just concrete.

'Should we empty the car now?' Mum said through a yawn, breaking that magical moment.

We carried boxes of provisions down from the car, and this time when we crossed its threshold the house had a more friendly, familiar feel about it.

'I could murder a mug of tea, how about you?' she said, squeezing past me into the tiny kitchenette. 'Lordy, check this out. Am I supposed to cook on this?' The oven door of the antique cooker gave a stiff creak when she opened it. She lifted a lighter gadget hanging on a hook at the side and snorted, 'Jings! I haven't seen one of those things since I was a bairn growing up here!'

'What is it?' I drew my eyebrows together.

'It works with a flint. You squeeze it like this,' she said, turning on the gas and clicking the gadget. It sparked and lit the gas.

'Cool,' I remarked. Soon we had a pizza in the oven and the kettle whistling on the hob.

'I'll get the fire going. You'll find tea bags in this box. Be a good lass, can you make us tea?' She handed me two mugs.

We cosied up together on the couch which she'd covered with a clean throw. It was kind of nice sprawled out on the old burst sofa in front of the fire, toasting our feet on the fender.

'More pizza?' Mum offered me the last slice.

'No thanks. I'm full,' I lied, feeling generous. 'You can have it.' She wolfed it down and gave a contented sigh.

'That feels better. I thought tomorrow we could drive into Stromness to shop. It's the school holidays here, and I could delay job hunting for a couple of weeks so we both have time to fix this place up. How about we make the house our holiday project?' She glanced over for my reaction.

'You mean there are actual shops here?' I teased.

'Of course, there's shops here, dafty!' She laughed. 'You're going to need more than your hoodie to keep out the elements in this northern climate. Tomorrow we'll get you a decent anorak, and welly boots …'

'Wooah!' I interrupted. 'No way am I wearing an anorak and welly boots. I'd look a proper nerd!'

'I'm just saying we'll get ourselves kitted out tomorrow. You can pick which bedroom you want and we'll buy paint …'

'Thanks, Mum,' I cut her off, 'but can we talk about it tomorrow. I'm so, so tired.' I yawned.

'Yeah.' She stretched out her arms. 'Me too, darlin.' We rolled out the sleeping bags.

'Pick. Which one do you want?' she asked.

'The one that doesn't smell of cheesy feet,' I said.

'OK.' She laughed chucking the blue one at me. 'Here you go.'

'This is like having a girlie sleepover, isn't it?' she said, giggling.

It felt so nice snuggling into the sleeping bag's warmth. I had barely replied before the shush, shush, shushing of the incoming tide lapping the shoreline lulled me off to sleep.

Later that night a haunting sorrowful sobbing sound came from the sea disturbing my sleep. Hearing the latch on the front door quietly closing, I roused myself and stood watching from the window as my mum stealthily left the house and padded barefoot down the moonlit beachtowards the ocean. She shrugged off her nightgown and slid silently into the sea. I stood for a while contemplating her pale form glide in and out through the white-crested waves.

Chapter 4

Noisy, squawking gulls woke me. Still half adrift in sleep, I pushed myself up and cast my eyes around. A glimmer of daylight struggling through the small grimy windows illuminated the sitting room in early, pale-yellow light. I stretched my cold legs feeling stiff from sleeping on the hard floor. My mum's gentle snoring reassured me. I guess she'd come back from her midnight swim after I'd fallen asleep again. Sliding out of my sleeping bag I pulled on my hoodie over my pyjamas and slipped into my trainers. Making as little noise as possible, I stepped out into the misty morning and quietly pulled the front door closed.

It felt good to stand a moment on the front step breathing in deep lungfuls of fresh salty sea air. A brisk breeze lifted my hair as I wandered down the garden path which led me through a rickety gate directly onto the shore. I liked the feel of soft white sand under my feet and felt a stab of hope. This was a brand-new start for us. Yeah. It's true Mum and I had made a few new starts in our time, but this time it felt different. This time we would settle down for good. I listened to the hypnotic murmur of the outgoing tide's gentle woosh ...woosh ... woosh washing over the sand. Having a wide expanse of empty beach on my doorstep gave me a surge of happiness. I kicked off my trainers and splashed through seaweed-covered rockpools stooping every now and again to fill my pockets with pretty white pebbles and pieces of opaque green and blue coloured glass worn smooth by the tides.

I paddled to the foreshore over wet wave-grooved sand to a cluster of large rocks, and finding a comfy hollow to lean into I hunkered down clasping my arms round my knees and gazed out to the silver line of the horizon. A shimmering mist hung over the ocean giving the sea a mystical unworldly quality. What would it sound like to hear a mermaid's song drifting across the ocean in the early-morning breeze? I wondered. The calm sea and peaceful early morning soothed me, making the sinister seabird's attack of the previous day seem nothing more than a bad dream.

I saw the dog first. A huge fierce-looking grey creature sniffing around clumps of washed-up seaweed. It bounded excitedly in and out of the surf, exuberantly shaking water droplets from its thick coat. I watched awhile and noticed it abruptly stop its frolicking, and, pricking its ears, it stood stock still as if heeding a command. Scanning the shoreline, I saw a shadowy dark figure emerge from the pearly morning haze. A tall, thin, slightly stooped woman wearing a long black coat strode purposefully along the shore, her face part hidden, muffled by a silver-white scarf.

The big dog stopped its frisking and immediately came to heel, walking obediently by her side. My calm mood evaporated when I realised they were heading in my direction. As they drew closer, I jumped up to leave. The woman held her hand up. 'Wait! It is you I have come to see.'

My heart leapt. 'W...Who me?' I stuttered.

'Aye! You, my bairn.' She had the same lilting accent as my mother.

In moments her black silhouette loomed over me.

'No need to be afraid, child,' she soothed, seeing the fright in my eyes. She placed a reassuring hand on my shoulder and continued in a gentle tone. 'You are Vanilia Solveig, are you not? Your mother is Rona Solveig.'

Unable to speak, I gave a slight nod.

'I thought so. The likeness to him is uncanny.' She held me in her gaze. 'Your father, Magnus Solveig, was my son. I am your grandmother.'

Standing back from me a little, she touched my face with the tips of her fingers.

'Child, you are the image of him.' Her eyes lingered on my face. 'You have your father's wild red hair, and' – her voice grew tender – 'you have his eyes.'

Soft early-morning sunlight gave way to the first strong rays of the day, capturing her in a pool of sunshine. Now I could see her clearly, I realised what I'd assumed to be a silver scarf was in fact her long silver-white hair which now blew around her face, partially obscuring it. As she pushed it aside, I saw she looked old but not withered. Her face lit up in a radiant smile. The deep, crinkly laughter lines etched around her sea-green eyes gave her a kindly look. Still lost for words, I took the hand she offered then jerked mine back flinching from the powerful static shock of electricity that sparked between us.

'Ah!' she laughed. 'There's nae doot you and I are connected.'

'As we walked up the beach together to the cottage, I asked, 'What's your dog's name?'

'It's Wolfie,' she replied. At the sound of his name the big dog looked up at me with tawny yellow eyes.

'What kind of dog is he?' I supposed from his size he must be a Husky crossed with Alsatian.

'Och, he's no' a dog,' she replied. 'He is a wolf.'

'An actual wolf!' I stared at him.

'Aye.' She nodded. 'He's a full-bred Canis lupus. He and I have been together for a very long time, haven't we, my bonny laddie?' The wolf nudged his nose under her hand, and she stroked his big head.

'And talking of names,' she continued, 'will you call me Granny or by my name, Aurora?'

'Aurora. That's if you don't mind?' I glanced at her, feeling shy.

'Aurora it is!' She linked her arm through mine. 'And you prefer to be known as Lia.'

I was bewildered. How could she know that?

'Now,' she said, 'let's go up to see your mother.' As we approached the house, I had a feeling it would be best if I ran ahead to warn Mum.

'Hang on. I'll just go ahead to let my mum know you're coming.'

'Very good,' Aurora replied as I sprinted off. Bursting through the cottage door I shouted, 'Mum, we've got a visitor.'

She was up and dressed. She'd raked over the embers of the fire and rekindled it. The room felt snug and warm. She sat perched in the window recess, her hands cupped around a mug of coffee.

'It's Aurora,' I whispered, nervous to see her reaction.

'I know. I watched you both come up the beach.' She nodded, her expression unreadable.

Pulling her coat from the peg on the door, she stepped out to greet my grandmother. I watched them from the window as the two gave each other an awkward hug and stood exchanging a few words. I couldn't contain my curiosity any longer and stepped out to join them.

'Aurora's invited us for supper tonight,' Mum said, looking flustered.

Aurora pointed along the coast to the town.

'I bide in that white hoose.' She indicated a large two-storey house, set apart from the other houses standing behind the harbour wall. She was about to say more when the heavens opened and rain started to pelt down.

'Sorry,' my mum apologised, 'we're not quite ready for visitors yet. There's nowhere clean to give you a seat.' She covered her head with her arms to shield herself from the downpour.

'No matter, dearie.' Aurora turned away, grumbling: 'Ach, this blashy weather. Go inside, the pair of you. You're getting soaked. I'll look forward to your visit to me later. I'll mak' a good pot of lamb broth.'

Mum held up her hands. 'Aurora, I should tell you we're vegetarians We don't eat meat.'

'Aye weel. I'll mak' a pot of Cullen skink. You'll eat fish soup, won't you?'

33

Avoiding the puddles which had quickly formed, she pulled her coat around her and turned to go, remarking with a grin, 'Wan thing you can say aboot wur weather here is there's no shortage of variety.'

'I like her,' I said when Mum and I were alone. 'And she has a tame wolf, that's pretty amazing!'

Mum nodded, towel-drying her hair. 'Aye, Aurora's a character, that's for sure. There's a lot more to her than meets the eye.'

'How do you mean?' I asked, burning with curiosity.

'Well, she's not like most people.' Mum paused, struggling to find the words. 'She's sort of, what I mean to say is, well she's a bit different. Och, I'm not explaining this very well, am I? Look …' – she checked out the window – 'the rain's gone off. Let's go a walk along the beach to have this talk.' She fetched my jacket. 'You're quite right you're of an age to know some family truths and secrets. It's been difficult for me to talk about your father's death, but there are things you have to know now.'

The talk of Granny Aurora being a bit different from other people made me want to confide my own worries to her. Taking a deep breath, I blurted out. 'Mum, there's stuff I need to talk over with you, too.'

She sank back down into the window nook seat.

'Tell me. What things, Lia?'

'Things that have been happening to me. It's hard to explain. Changes. Powerful feelings I don't understand. I'm confused and a bit sc ...'

Distracted by something she saw through the window, Mum laid my jacket down again.

'Ach. Sorry, pet, this talk will have to wait until later.'
'But, Mum...'
She pointed to some men carrying a heavy sofa down the track. 'Look. Our furniture's arrived.'

Chapter 5

We had a hectic afternoon, with no time for chat as we unpacked box after box. Mum groaned.

'Ach, I should have given half of this stuff to charity. 'Why on earth did I pack that?' she grimaced, pulling out a garden barbeque. 'We'll not use it here very often!'

Somehow we found a home for everything. I made endless cups of tea while she directed the removal men on where to place our furniture. They were great. They even uplifted the old battered settee and chair. We worked our socks off cleaning and shifting stuff around and generally making the house feel like a home. I chose the bedroom tucked away on its own. OK, it's small but it gives me my own private space and I love that it has a sweeping view of the beach and ocean.

Mum shook out the duvet then flopped down on the bed. 'That's your bedroom sorted. Let's leave it for now, Lia. We've done enough. I'm just so happy we'll get a comfortable sleep tonight.'

'Mum. Late last night I was woken by a strange noise. It sounded like sobbing coming from the sea. I saw you from the window out on the bay swimming in the moonlight.'

'Ah,' she said with a hint of a frown, 'what you heard were

the seals out in the bay. Their calls can sound quite eerie at night. Sorry I woke you. I couldn't sleep so I went for a swim. You never know,' – the corners of her mouth quirked up – 'one day I might find myself swimming with the Selkie folk.' There was a wistfulness in her voice.

My brow puckered. 'The Selkie folk?'

'Aye. The Seal people,' she said in a matter-of-fact-tone. 'They live in wild coastal waters. They're said to be a gentle race and' – she raised her eyebrows – 'they have a secret.'

'What's their secret?' I asked, fascinated.

Her eyes flickered. 'It's said people who drowned at sea are turned into seals but, on just one night of the year, they can remove their skins and take a human form again. On that particular night, midsummer's night, the Selkie folk can come ashore and communicate with people on land.'

'You said that as if it were true.' I stared at her. 'Surely that's just in fables? Are you telling me the Selkie folk actually exist?

She merely gazed back at me, a mysterious smile playing on her lips.

Later that afternoon while in the car driving along the seafront road to Aurora's home, I said, 'Orkney's a special place, isn't it, Mum. I can feel it.'

'Aye, it is, darlin'.' she agreed. 'It's a place of ancient and modern. There's a respect for the old pagan ways and customs but also an eagerness to grasp the future.'

We drove into a little town of narrow cobbled streets where shops and houses huddled together against wind and weather. The main road took us down to a quaint, colourful working harbour where boats bobbed and jostled each other at the quayside. The setting sun mingled with the soft streetlights casting everything in a warm golden glow. Mum stopped the car, and we sat by the sea wall lost in the moment.

'Ahh, isn't that a bonnie sunset?' she sighed. 'They call this the golden hour.'

A mouth-watering smell of fish and chips drifted over to us from the Harbour Café on the front, reminding us we were hungry.

Mum stirred. 'Come on, I'm starving. Let's go up to Aurora's for supper.'

Aurora's house stood sheltered by the sea wall accessed by a single-track road along the front. Wolfie bounded down the garden path to meet us. I took a step back, frightened by his size, but soon realised I needn't have worried: he was a big softy. He was wagging his whole back end and I would swear he smiled at me. Oh, not in a human way but he bared his teeth in a wide doggy grin bidding me welcome. Aurora followed him out, holding a lantern high to light our way.

'Welcome, bairns. Welcome!' She guided us in. 'Come away in, dearies. Drat! Mind an' no trip over Wolfie's bed; it taks up most of this wee porch.'

Too late! I stumbled over it in the dark. A peculiar smell wrinkled my nose the moment we stepped into her shadowy hallway.

'It's fish oil,' Mum whispered. 'She doesn't have

electricity. She lights her home with oil lamps and candles.'

'No way!' I blurted.

'Shush!' Mum gave me one of her looks.

Aurora fussed around us, ushering us into her big flag-stoned kitchen. A smell of wood smoke drifted towards us from a roaring fire crackling in a black-lead fireplace. Drawn into its warmth I stretched my hands out to its heat while Aurora busied herself poking the red glowing embers and stirring a big pot of soup bubbling on the lead range.

'Tak a seat, lasses.' She placed a little three-legged stool in front of me. 'And sit yourself doon there, Rona.' Mum lifted Aurora's knitting and settled herself into a comfy winged armchair by the fire. While Aurora set the table with a freshly baked loaf, a slab of cheddar cheese, oatcakes, butter in a dish, plates, knives and spoons and a little dish of tablet my curious eyes explored the room. There were no pictures on the whitewashed walls except for a framed embroidered sampler hanging above the fireplace. In small neat stitching, it read:

LANG MAY YOUR LUM REEK
AND YOUR KAIL POT BOIL.

A little table beside me had books of sheet music lying open and a fiddle propped against it. I touched the fiddle, running my fingers over its smooth polished surface.

'Ye may hold it if you like.' Aurora said, handing it to me with a smile. 'Playing the fiddle is a long tradition in our family.' Her face lit up. 'I could teach you to play, Lia? Would you like that?'

'Yes, please!' I felt thrilled. 'I would love to learn to play the fiddle.' I held the bow lightly.

'Your granny is a very fine fiddle player,' my mum said with a smile. 'Whenever there's a wedding or a party she's the first one to be invited.'

'Aye,' Aurora laughed. 'That is true, Rona. In fact, I am soon to travel to Eynenholme Island to play my fiddle at the Ostara celebrations.

'What's Ostara?' I asked.

'Weel …' She stroked her chin. '… It's a celebration to welcome spring. Look. Come over here. I'll show you.'

She unrolled a yellowed parchment scroll and spread it out over the floor. Kneeling over it she explained: 'This is the Wheel of the Year. It marks the seasonal cycles. It's shaped like a wheel, you see.' She traced her long tapering fingers round the markings on its circle. 'Here is Yule in December. Imbolc in February, Ostara in March, Beltane in May. Litha in June is Midsummer. Mabon in September. You will know Sahmain in October as Halloween. Sahmain ushers in the dark half of the year.

'Yeah!' I interrupted. 'I love Halloween. Last year I dressed up as a scary witch.'

She glanced up, giving me a strange look. 'Oh, gracious,' she said, raising her hands to us. 'My poor old knees. Help me up, dears.'

'It's a kind of calendar, isn't it?' I said as I helped her to her feet.

'Aye. It's a calendar which marks the old pagan festivals which our people still ...'

Mum abruptly changed the subject. 'It would be good for you to learn to play an instrument, Lia. The sound of a fiddle is a merry sound indeed.' She took the fiddle from me and handed it back to Aurora. 'Play for us, won't you? Please, Aurora.'

Aurora took the fiddle and smiled. 'Of course I will, with the greatest of pleasure.' She tucked the fiddle under her chin and drew back its bow. Tapping her foot to keep time to the music she played a lively jig. The sound of her fiddling, warm, dark, bright and sweet transported me to a place that felt magical. It was like the sea on a fine spring day, sparkling with sunshine. When she finished we gave her an enthusiastic round of applause.

'Thank you, Aurora,' I marvelled. 'That was beautiful. How soon can I start my lessons?'

41

Wolfie padded over to us and stretching out he made himself comfortable on the fireside rug, sprawling himself over Aurora's feet.

'Och move, Wolfie, you great lump. You're the giddy limit!' she said, laying her fiddle aside and pulling her feet out from under him.

'You've got such interesting things,' I said, pointing to a spinning wheel tucked into the window recess. It intrigued me. 'Do you use your spinning wheel, Aurora, or is it kind of an antique?'

'Oh, I use it. I spin sheep's wool into yarn and I knit.' She picked up her knitting needles. 'I will knit you a fine warm jumper.' Raising her finger, she cautioned. 'No matter if it's summer or winter in Orkney, you will need to wear plenty of woollens to keep oot the chill!'

I toasted my feet at the fire. 'Do you have a proper cooker or do you only have your fire to cook on?' I asked, fascinated.

Mum interrupted me with a frown. 'Lia, don't ask so many questions.'

'Sorry, I don't mean to be bad-mannered,' I apologised. 'It's just I've never been to a house like this. It feels like I've time-travelled into the past.'

Mum smiled. 'I guess you haven't moved with the times, have you, Aurora?'

Aurora's mouth twitched. 'Indeed, in many ways I have not! The old ways are good, but I am not set in them, Rona. We must keep up with the world's great progression.' Turning to me, she pondered, 'What would you say to this idea, Lia? I will teach you to play the fiddle and you will teach me the wonders of the computer. They tell me it is a miraculous fountain of knowledge. I am very interested in experimenting with its magic. The only

42

technology I have is an old typewriter left here after the war, or should I say – the way I type – a typewronger!

Laughing, I held my hand up to her in a high five but the gesture was completely lost on her. 'It's a deal,' I agreed. 'I'll teach you how to surf the web.'

'Surf the web?' she said with a mystified look. 'Many years ago as a child I surfed the waves so I expect I could learn to surf a web.' Turning back to the fire, she answered my question. 'You asked if I use my range for cooking and the answer is yes. I use it for cooking and for the warmth of course and drying my socks.' She pointed to a line of woollen socks hanging from a brass rail fixed to the mantelpiece.

Lifting each of the three bowls warming at the fireplace in turn, she ladled them full with steaming soup. 'Now, dear,' she said, placing the bowls on a tray, 'help me carry this over.' She followed me over to the table carrying a plate of warm flatbread rounds.

'You must try those. They're delicious. She set them down in front of us. 'Bere bannocks made from Orkney's own good grain. Come, lasses, sit yourselves doon.' We pulled in our chairs around the big circular wooden table. Handing us each a glass, mine filled with elderberry cordial and Mum's with homemade heather ale, she raised her own glass.

'I make a toast to family,' she said and we raised our glasses.

'To family.'

'Now tuck in, bairns, and enjoy.' She placed bowls of thick steaming soup down in front of us. 'I'm fair enjoying this, Aurora. You make the best Cullen skink on the island.' Mum helped herself to another ladleful.

'Yeah. It's yummy,' I agreed, and finishing my second helping of the delicious creamy fish soup, I cleaned my plate with a hunk of crusty bread.

'Ah! You are indeed your father's daughter!' Aurora smiled, scraping the last drop into my bowl. 'How Magnus loved to eat my fish soup.' A look of sadness passed between my mother and Aurora.

'Come,' Aurora stood up. 'If we're finished eating, let's go ben to my "siterooterie".' She lit a candle and led us from the kitchen through the hall to a glass-fronted sunroom which had a wonderful panoramic view over the rocky beach to the sea beyond. Wolfie followed us in and settled himself at Aurora's feet. I flopped down in her wicker chair, my eyes scanning the bay which was softly lit by a canopy of twinkling stars. I felt a definite frisson of magic in the air.

† 𝓧 ⊼ ⊠ †

Aurora leaned towards me. 'Your mother and I have spoken and agreed it's time to tell you the truth about our past, Lia, but before I begin I have a gift for you.' She placed a polished pearly clamshell in my lap. Look inside.'

I prised it opened with eager fingers. Inside, to my delight, I found an exquisite necklace. I held it by its delicate silver chain, admiring the way the light caught its beautiful luminous blue-green stone. Its colours shimmered and shifted like the ocean.

'It's an aquamarine,' she explained. 'A jewel

from the sea. It is the treasure of mermaids. Its stone inspires truth and trust, and it's a talisman for good luck. It belonged to me as a girl and now it is my gift to you.' She fastened its clasp around my neck.

'Thank you,' I said, touching the stone. 'I love it. I'll always wear it.'

'Good lass.' She gave me a smile that lit up her face and leaning forward she met my eyes.

'I know you're confused – even frightened – by the recent changes you've become aware of in yourself, Lia.'

I blushed and said nothing.

'I want to help you to find yourself, Lia, and to do that it's important you know about your past. Learning about our family history will help you to truly understand who you are.'

She picked up her knitting and, making herself comfortable, gazed out over the bay and began her story.

Chapter 6

'I was born at exactly the stroke of midnight on midsummer's night in the year 1625.'

'Did you say 1625?' I interrupted. 'Is this is an Orcadian folk tale, Aurora?'

'No, Vanilia.' She shook her head. 'This is not a tale.' She leaned across and patted my hand. 'I am telling you the truth.' She held up her hand and continued.

'I saw the light of day at that late hour because here on our islands the sun doesn't set in midsummer. You must know I was not born a mortal.' Her eyes flickered over mine. 'I was born a mermaid into a community of sea people. My mother gave birth to me in the depths of the ocean where the darkness is such that you could not tell where it ended and the rocky seabed began.

'"A girl," my mother announced, hoping my father would not be disappointed. My father did not mind his first child being a daughter. He swam with me to the upper world, and breaking through the waves he held me up in the twilight of midsummer's night. "My firstborn. My daughter. You will belong to the four elements, Earth, Air, Fire, and Water." Giving me his blessing he named me Aurora.'

'Are you actually telling me you started your life centuries ago as a mermaid?' I stared at her, disbelieving.

Mum shushed me. 'Please just listen, Lia!'

Aurora lit another candle. As its subtle flame rose and flared, I felt the real world fall away and I believed absolutely that on this enchanted island anything could be possible.

Aurora placed her hand on her heart. 'Yes. I was born a mermaid.'

And when she fixed her sea-green eyes on mine, I saw in them the depths of the ocean and in that moment I knew she spoke the truth.

'As a child, I lived in Finfolkaheem, a fine city under the sea. Ah, Lia,' Aurora sighed, 'It was a place of wondrous beauty. My younger sister, Tyra, and I were inseparable. She was as dear to me as my own life. We passed our childhood days playing tag together, darting through softly waving seagrasses, speaking to fish and learning how to coax drops from the clouds and calm restless surging tides. We plitered and bathed in bubbling sea-spume and rode the crests of white-capped waves with pretty, laughing water nymphs. Although they were fair, my sister Tyra's beauty outshone them all. Her skin had the luminosity of pink translucent seashells. Her eyes reflected the deep turquoise sea. Her lips were tinted the rosy red of coral, and her hair, which was her great vanity, hung down her back in waves of spun gold.

'Once when our mother was brushing her hair with ivory combs she happened to remark, "My bonny lass you will make a fair match."

'"How fair?" Tyra asked, posing prettily.

'"You will marry a mortal," my mother replied.
'Our youthful dreams were all of becoming brides. We set our sights on marrying a human husband, understanding that, if a mermaid married a mortal she could live on land

47

with him as a white witch or spey-wife and be respected by her community for her gifts of healing. She would be known to use her powers for the good of humankind but she would never be one of them. She would not die as mortals die; she would be immortal. However,' – Aurora raised her finger – 'Tyra and I knew that the alternative to marrying a human would be to marry a fin-man, which has very different consequences. Fin-wives are ill-treated and soon lose their beauty, their fate is to become hideous crones, condemned to a life on land as malevolent evil witches … reviled and cast out. They are known to use their powers to create havoc and destruction. They are feared and shunned.'

Aurora looked at me with sharp intelligent eyes. 'There is a powerful connection between witches and faeries, and a constant tug of war between good and evil.'

'When you were growing up as a mermaid, did you have a fishtail, Aurora?'

Mum shot me a look but I couldn't resist asking,

'Ah.' The corners of her mouth curled. 'People believe mermaids had fishtails, but no. We wore petticoats embroidered with blue-green and silver threads. We tied them at the ankles for swimming. Ah, but if a mermaid could persuade a mortal man to fall in love with her, then she had the power to lay aside her petticoat 'tail' for ever.'

'Did you persuade a mortal man to fall in love with you, Aurora?'

'Wheesht!' Her smile faded. 'I'm coming to that. Let me tell my story in my own way, Lia.'

Holding my tongue, I resolved not to interrupt her again.

'Erland Dreever was the most handsome man in the whole of Orkney. His auburn hair, green eyes and red beard

caused many young lasses to gaze on him with admiring eyes, including my sister who was determined to marry a mortal man. She thought to charm and lure him with her sweet voice, plotting to draw him to her like a fish to a hook. One morning early, while he was out fishing near to the shore, Erland heard Tyra's song carried to him on a soft breeze. It filled his senses and intoxicated him. Transfixed he stared in wonder at the mermaid whom he now saw sitting on a rock singing and combing out her long golden hair. He thought her the most beautiful woman he had ever seen in his life. In that moment he fell in love with her and called out to her.

'"Marry me now, my beauty, and come and live with me on land. I have a fine farm with a good stock of cattle and sheep."

'Tyra answered him. "Yes, I will marry you, but I cannot come and live in your cold land with your black rain and white snow. I can't live with your icy wind and frost and smoky fires. No. You must come and live with me in Finfolkaheem. Come with me to my home under the sea. There is no wind or rain on my land. We can live there in peace and happiness forevermore."

'Erland shook his head as if emerging from a trance. He slowly turned away from Tyra and rowed back to the shore. My sister wept and wailed at her foolishness. She knew she had forever forfeited the chance of marrying a mortal. I tried to console her but she refused to speak of him. She howled like a banshee if his name was mentioned. After a time she shut herself away in a dark sea-cave refusing to see anyone.

'Erland had a fiddle. One fine summer's evening, just for the love of it, he took a walk down to the foreshore and began to play, but this day it proved to be a dangerous thing to do. Firstly he had forgotten that it was midsummer's day.' Aurora set aside her knitting and folded her hands into her lap, 'Faerie folk,' she explained, 'have their greatest power at midsummer and midwinter, Lia. Secondly, he was standing on the shoreline between high and low water. This is a place where the devil and all supernatural creatures have great power because it is neither a part of land nor part of the sea. Standing below the tide mark playing his finest set of reels and jigs Erland soon noticed he wasn't alone. An old man, grey-haired and whiskered, emerged from the ocean and waded towards him.'

'"Well," said the man, "That was very fine playing. Tell me. Would you be good enough to come and play for me and my friends? We're celebrating midsummer's night."

Erland knew he was speaking to a trow but he was afraid to refuse, knowing the danger he would be in. He accepted, and the old man led him out into deep waters.

'The sea began to foam and churn. Erland felt himself being sucked under the waves. He knew he had been tricked and was meant to drown. Just as he gave himself up to his fate he gazed down into the deep dark waters and caught a glimpse of me swimming far below. I swam up to him, and breaking the surface I wrapped my hands around the back of his neck to support him and swam him to the shore. Standing unsteadily in the shallows, he fell into my arms bewitched. Thanking me for his life, he kissed me.

'"Will you come with me and live with me on land

and be my wife. I have a fine farm with livestock where we can be happy."

'Overjoyed, I readily agreed to be his wife and live on the land with him.' Aurora's expression saddened and she shook her head. 'I had no idea this was the same man who had rejected my sister.'

'It was the talk of the whole island. Erland Dreever has asked some strange lass who nobody knew to marry him. After we wed, we had a party. Erland played the fiddle, and I danced the whole night long as light as a feather. I outshone all of the local lasses.'

A shadow passed over Aurora's face. 'Everyone wished us well apart from one – my sister Tyra. When she discovered I was to marry Erland she was filled with fury. She raged to all who would listen. Spreading false tales, sobbing of my betrayal and treachery.

'She swore I had stolen the man who rightfully belonged to her. She would not admit that it was she who had forfeited her chance to be Erland's bride. She vowed she would never forgive me and swore she would have her revenge.

'So your sister became your enemy?'

'Yes!' Aurora shuddered. 'I tried to go to her, sure she would listen to me, sure I could convince her it was never my intention to cause her any hurt, but she had disappeared.

Her eyes glistened. 'I heard she had married a fin-man. Oh, I feared for her. They are an evil-hearted, unholy race. Dark, silent, moody, amphibious men who are skilled sorcerers known to have power over the skies and seas. Storm-raisers.' My granny frowned.

'Word of my sister came to me. I heard she suffered greatly from this fin-man's cruelty. When he died she had to give up her life in the sea, and she came to live on land in a small derelict cottage on the shores of a vanishing island. Because she had lived so long apart from the rest of the community, she had come to expect neither kindness nor a word of comfort from any quarter.' Aurora paused, tears shimmering in her eyes. 'Tyra withdrew into herself. She shunned the sea people's company. For many days she didn't cross the threshold of her cottage. She blocked out her windows and sat alone in the dark. Some said they saw her sitting by her fire, her arms wrapped around herself, rocking back and forth singing a sad lament. I felt her desolation. I wept for her.'

Aurora's face clouded. 'I remembered her as a girl. Our heads bent together laughing over some mischief we were hatching. I couldn't abandon her. The following morning I rowed to her island intending to bring her home. A cloying mist closed in, wet and heavy. My sixth sense warned me as I neared the shallows that she had sensed my coming and meant to do me harm. I turned and rowed back out to sea. When I glanced back I saw my sister standing on the shore, a grey ghost, her hair lank, her eyes like dead empty holes. I saw her face contort in rage as she screamed an ear-splitting scream.

'"Sister, I curse you and your line for ever."

'I stood up unsteadily in the boat and called out to her: '"Tyra, my sister. It was never my intention to do you harm. When will you forgive me?"

In a bloodcurdling shriek, her bitter words carried

53

to me on the wind.

'"I will never forgive you. Your pain, sorrow and destruction will be my whole reason to exist."

'She plunged into the sea, her face twisted in hate, and with a powerful stroke swam swiftly towards my boat. I barely had time to grab up the oars.

'I rowed with all of my strength, the sound of her howling frustration and vile curses in my ears. Snatching a look back, I saw Tyra sink down into the deep ocean. Only her eyes were visible above the surface, watching me. Then, to my horror, in a great burst of sea-spume, she resurfaced in the form of a hideous many headed sea-monster, spurting water from flaring nostrils. I cowered down in my flimsy vessel while the creature stretched out its long spiked tentacles. With an unearthly clamour, it began circling my boat, making ringed waves that formed a maelstrom to suck me under.

'I yelled into the wind, "Save me!" The breeze picked up in strong gusts catching at my little boat. The wash of a great wave pushed it forward in a great surge, taking me out of harm's reach. When I reached the shallows I hauled my boat onto the shore knowing we would never be with each other again as sisters. I was not sorry. To think I had once adored and loved her, my little sister Tyra who had transformed herself into a hideous monster by her own hate and venom.

Chapter 7

'Was it Tyra who brought about my father's death, Aurora?'

She moved across to the window and gazed silently out into the night. When she finally spoke her voice had a slight tremor.

'Not long after my terrifying encounter with my sister, Tyra was seen by a fisherman who was walking the Yesnaby coast. He saw her on the Black Craig cliffs kneeling precariously on the cliff edge, the waves thundering below. She was chanting incantations, invoking a spell to call up a mighty storm. It's said she was communing with the devil. In return for this favour, she vowed to do his wicked work for all eternity. As soon as she'd uttered her promise, the wind picked up with savage ferocity whipping the sea into a violent raging storm.'

Aurora stiffened. 'That night Tyra fulfilled her vow to pay me back. She took her terrible revenge on me but' – her mouth set in a hard line – 'her actions also had grave consequences for her.'

A chill ran through me. 'What happened to her?'

Aurora continued gazing out into the dark night.

'She was banished for ever.'

As Aurora spoke, creeping clouds blotted out the moon and a draught of cold air extinguished the candle, pitching us into complete darkness.

'Who banished her? Where is she?' I whispered, shuddering.

Aurora relit the candle and clasped her hands in her lap.

'That is an interesting story. At that time my world was changing. The faerie folk disliked the intrusion of civilisation into their habitat. Conflict between humans and faeries drove the faerie folk underground. They hid in caves and mountain recesses and split into two groups. The Seelie Court and the Unseelie Court. The Seelie Court aligned itself with Mother Nature. They are benevolent spirits. They continue to exist to this day, living on land to do only good and no harm. Their desire is to coexist in peace with the human race.

'The Unseelie Court is hostile to humans. They survive underground. They are a malevolent, demonic people, focusing all their efforts on injury, terror and destruction – even to the extermination of mortals.' Her eyes hardened.

'My sister Tyra was banished because of her wickedness. She fled underground. She is now ruler over the Unseelie Court. Her kingdom is concealed in subterranean caves on the vanishing island of Elfhame.' Aurora hung her head. 'Tyra has embraced evil and is entirely wicked.' A flush crept up her neck. 'She exists to cause harm to the world. I use my magic for good; she uses her magic for evil.'

'You have magical powers, Aurora?' I stared at her.

'Yes. Though no one can prove the existence of magic, and people's beliefs in such things have changed over time, I am here as proof that the mortal world's connection with the faerie world is still a close one.'

She gazed out over the ocean. 'At times, during the summer months, you can just see the ghostly outline of Tyra's phantom island shrouded in mist suspended above the ocean.'

'Phantom island? What does that mean?' I asked her.

She gazed out to the horizon. 'It's an island that isn't marked on any map but which from time to time appears where there should be no land.'

Unsettled and frightened by her story, I moved over to sit by Mum, who curled her arms around me and pulled me close.

'Have you ever gone back to Findfolkaheem, Aurora?' I asked.

'No, Lia,' she replied. 'I no longer belong to the sea. I chose to live my life on the land but sadly' – she glanced down –'there are complications arising out of the arrangement of marriage between mortals and faerie folk. I was a good land-wife to Erland. I brewed the best ale on the islands. I spun and knitted, baked and cooked. Our son Magnus's birth completed our happiness.' She reached over and squeezed my mum's hand. 'But the sad truth is humans have a much shorter lifespan than we faerie folk. After your grandfather Erland died, I had to decide for the sake of my son who could not breathe underwater to remain living on land, but, although I live with human folk, I am not one of them.

'If you're no longer a mermaid and you're not a mortal, then what are you?' I asked.

She leaned forward, levelling a steady gaze on me.

'I am a witch.'

'Y ... you're a witch?' I stammered, feeling the colour drain from my face.

'No, bairn.' Her eyes flickered. 'Don't be afraid of me. I am a "white witch."' I only ever used my powers for doing good.'

I shot a look at Mum. 'Does that mean you're a witch too. Have you been keeping it secret from me?'

She held my eyes. 'It's true magic also ran in my family. I was born with supernatural powers but I gave up my magic when we left Orkney. I was afraid it could lead Tyra to us and put us in danger. I've allowed my magic to wither. I do share Aurora's affinity with nature. We both care about protecting our planet, the ocean, wildlife and our ecosystem but Aurora uses magic to help safeguard it. I now use science.'

'I need to hear it all now, Mum,' I said, curling into her. 'Tell me, how my father died and why did we leave Orkney?'

Aurora and my mother exchanged a look.

'Yes. It's time you knew, Lia.' My mum stroked my hair. 'We didn't leave Orkney … we fled!

She broke off, fighting back tears.

Aurora pressed her fingers to her lips. 'Shh … shush … Rona. Let me tell it.' She turned towards me.

'Your mother took you far away from this place to protect you.'

This revelation made me sit bolt upright. 'What do you mean?' I stared at her.

'Wheesht, child. Let me speak and I will tell you all. Magnus was a good son and a good man. Everyone knew that he and your mother, Rona, would marry. Many men tried to win her as their bride but' – she glanced over at my mother – 'You didn't want any of those other men did you, Rona?' Aurora turned back to me. 'Your mother had fallen in love with my son and he with her.' We booked

the kirk and paid the minister. The cog was made to toast
the happy couple.'

'On the day of the wedding, a sharp sweet odour
hung in the air, a warning of a coming storm. Folk from the
islands turned out in their best finery to attend the wedding
celebrations of Magnus and Rona. The little church bulged
at the seams with happy expectant guests, but at the very
moment the bride and groom took their vows all was
thrown into chaos. A deafening clap of thunder rang out
and a blinding flash illuminated the church. A silver streak
of forked lightning struck the steeple of the kirk. It burst
into flames. Pandemonium followed. Panicking wedding
guests stampeded from the church. They stood outside
in huddles, stricken, watching their church burn to the
ground.'

My mother flinched at the memory. Aurora gripped
the arm of her chair and continued: 'I knew without
a shadow of doubt that this wicked deed was Tyra's
doing. It was meant as a warning to show she cursed me
for marrying Erland and had not forgotten her vow of
vengeance against me.'

Chapter 8

Aurora frowned. 'From that day on my family lived in fear of Tyra's threat.'

'For that reason my son Magnus decided the day you were born to move away from the islands to keep his family safe. He found a little cottage on the mainland.' Her eyes softened at the memory. 'He worked hard to make it a fit and habitable home for you and your mother. His family meant everything to him. When fair weather came and conditions were right, he loaded his small boat and set sail with you and your mother to your new life. It broke my heart to see you go. I came down to the pier to wave you goodbye as he pushed the boat down to the sea. "Safe journey!" I called out as he sailed away, though what could go wrong on a beautiful calm summer day?' Her expression clouded. 'A dense sea-fog rolled in from nowhere obscuring visibility. It's murky veil enshrouded the boat, causing it to drift off course. Next, a howling wind sprung up. It whipped the sea into giant waves, lifting the little boat and driving it towards jagged rocks. As the storm raged on, pounding the cliffs, I ran down to the shore frantic for news of my family and joined the commotion and confusion on the beach. Folk were whispering of a witch's curse. They said my sister Tyra was in league with the devil, and accused her of raising the storm. An old fisherman, Fergus Rendall, spoke of the strange sight he had seen from his vantage point on the clifftop. He swore on that morning he witnessed my sister deranged and ragged, kneeling on the cliff edge before a dark sinister figure. He saw her raving before falling to the ground, clasping her hands in a begging gesture. A flash of lightning illuminated the stranger. Fergus Rendall swore that my sister had raised the devil himself. He saw with his own eyes how the mighty demon rose up, eyes flaring red, radiating evil.

'The spectre bellowed into the night, calling forth a mighty tempest. The wind howled around the apparition like a demented banshee. Tyra fell at the spirit's feet, prostrating herself, until it finally vanished in a great clap of thunder. Fergus Rendall's voice cracked as he described what came next. Deafening thunder rumbled and crashed. White-hot lightning bolts split open the sky. The sea boiled up like a seething cauldron.'

Aurora fixed her gaze on the darkening sky and spoke in a hushed tone.

'Tyra had been granted this favour, but, in return, she forfeited her soul.'

My mouth felt dry. I licked my lips and swallowed hard. 'Aurora, did my father die in a shipwreck?'

She held her finger to her lips.

'From his vantage point on the cliff, Fergus Rendall watched as your father's vessel was tossed back and forth in the heaving swell, driven towards the cliffs as if it were nothing more than a feather. Struggling to see through driving rain, he picked out a woman on board who had a small swaddled child tied to her back. He saw her leap overboard and disappear into the raging sea just before the ship was hurled against the rocks, splintering it into pieces. With a final huge tidal surge, the ship's wreckage was sucked down beneath the waves for ever. Fergus solemnly vowed he beheld something astounding occur. He gave his word of honour he witnessed four mermaids bear the woman and child up from the depths of the ocean. He watched dumbfounded as they carried her to safety, holding her above the waves through the churning sea. The mermaids swam her to the nearby deserted island of Fara. The fisherman watched them pull the woman into the shallows and lay her, together with the body of her baby, on the deserted shore.

Aurora paused for a moment and took a sip from her glass. 'Should I go on, Rona?' She tilted her head, waiting for an answer.

'Yes.' My mother nodded. 'Lia should hear it all.' Aurora came to sit by us. She took my hand and continued in a hushed tone.

'When the wind calmed, I was taken by boat to the uninhabited island of Fara. Just as the old fisherman had sworn, a young woman's body lay crumpled on the beach, a babe in her arms.

Aurora paused a moment composing herself, and clearing her throat she continued.

'I had convinced myself they were dead, but when I dropped to my knees beside them I felt a surge of hope. The baby gave a feeble whimper which stirred the woman into life. Spluttering and choking, she sat up and cradled her baby in her arms.

Aurora squeezed her eyes shut and clasped her hands together. 'I could hardly believe it – they had survived!'

When I glanced over to my mum and saw the look on her face, the truth struck me like a sledgehammer.

'It was us, wasn't it, Mum? It was you and I who survived that shipwreck!' She nodded, too upset to speak. 'But my father didn't survive, did he?'

Aurora let out a harsh breath. 'How could it have been possible for my son to have died?' She spoke almost under her breath, tears springing to her eyes. 'I believed Magnus was immortal, but that fateful day Tyra's malevolent arts prevailed. She turned my bright world dark.'

Aurora's care-worn face showed profound sadness. 'We never recovered his body. We searched and searched for him, but after a time we had to let go of our hope and accept he had perished.'

So that was how my father had died!

Aurora cleared her throat. 'I have to tell you more, I'm afraid, Lia. Your mother brought you back here to Orkney to keep you safe. We know you've inherited the gift of magic. Tyra fears that, as you grow older, your magic will strengthen and challenge hers. She sees you as her rival. Your powers are emerging. Controlling the elements for destructive purposes has sapped Tyra's strength. Her powers are diminishing.' Aurora leaned towards me. 'Before her powers weaken further, she means to rejuvenate her magic by stealing yours.'

'But how would she do that?' I flinched.

Aurora's eyes held mine. 'You are the last in our

line, Lia. If she could, she would enslave you and plunder your powers.'

I had a sudden frightening flashback. 'The storm. The sinister bird menacing me on the sea-crossing! That was a threat from Tyra!' I jolted upright. 'We can't stay here! It's not safe! We have to leave this island as soon as possible!'

'We can't run from her,' my mother said flatly, laying a restraining hand on my arm.

'I once believed I could keep you safe far from here, if we just kept moving, but it isn't so. Distance or location won't stop her. Her radar will find you wherever you go and she will not spare you.' Her hand tightened on my arm. 'The islands are the only place you can be safe, close to Aurora. She can protect you. That's why we came back, Lia. You have powerful inner magic, but you need to be taught how to wield it.'

'You knew I have supernatural powers, Mum?' I blushed.

Her calm eyes held mine. 'I've always known you've inherited the gift of magic. I knew when I strapped you as a tiny baby to my back and leapt from that sinking ship that your magic would protect you and that somehow you would survive, and sure enough my true friends the mermaids came to our rescue. You have extremely potent magic, Lia. I knew as you grew older it would surface. You've become aware of it, and it's troubled you. I think you've tried to talk to me about it haven't you. I'm sorry I didn't listen.'

'I felt scared to talk to you about it, Mum. I haven't told anyone. I've been so frightened of the feelings. I thought I could handle it by just disowning it. I hoped it would just go away.'

'Don't be afraid of it. It's as much a part of you as breathing.' Mum stroked my hair and kissed my head. 'Aurora will teach you how to use it for good purpose.'

'What about Tyra? Can she be stopped?' I trembled.

My mother's forehead creased. 'In her pact with the devil, Tyra gave up her immortality. She knows she can't survive for ever. You are young, Lia – your powers are rising. Tyra plans to revive her powers by stealing yours. No matter where we run, no matter where we hide, she will find us. She knows she has to replenish her magical powers soon or die. It will be up to you to stop her.'

My mother registered my stricken face and squeezed my shoulder. 'Don't worry, Lia. Aurora will keep you safe. She's a powerful witch.'

Aurora's eyes sparked. 'Aye. Long ago Tyra set herself against me, and now we are locked into an endless battle. She is a formidable adversary but she will not win because you, Lia, are destined to be the most powerful witch of all.'

Chapter 9

Aurora hurried from the room and came back holding a glass.

'Take a sip of this, bairn.'

'Aurora, that's whisky! You can't give her that! My mother scolded, snatching the glass from her.

'Och, sorry.' Aurora held up her palms. 'The lass looked like she needed something strong to steady her.'

'I'll be all right, I just felt dizzy for a moment,' I said, trying to get to my feet but wobbling precariously.

'Don't try to get up yet, Lia.' My mum passed a glass of water into my shaky hand.

'Sip this slowly, darlin'. This has all been a huge shock. You're shaking.'

Aurora fetched a warm woollen blanket and wrapped me in it, hovering over me. 'There now, bairn, take slow sips of the water.'

'That's good – the colour's coming back to your face,' Mum clucked, tucking the blanket around me. 'Do you feel any better, Lia?'

'Yes.' I nodded. 'I don't feel faint anymore.'

Aurora's shoulders slumped. 'It's all been too much for her, Rona. We should have waited until she was older.'

'No.' Mum placed her hand on Aurora's arm. 'We couldn't wait. Lia's at an age when she needs to know

67

everything.'

Another major panic attack threatened to overwhelm me. 'It isn't only Tyra I'm afraid of. It's my own powers. I don't know if I want magic in my life.'

Aurora took my hand. 'You have a choice, Lia. You don't have to take the path of magic, and if that is your decision, then in time your magic will wither and fade away. You will become as a mortal with no supernatural powers but' – her voice became laden with warning – 'Tyra will always be your enemy. Without magic, you will be helpless against her. For now, though, our combined magic is far too strong for her to be a real threat. To help make you feel safe I will give you Wolfie to guard you.'

As if he understood, the big dog padded over and sat beside me. I reached out and stroked his silky ears. He yawned lazily, then showing his big sharp teeth and putting his head in my lap, he gazed up at me with primal wolf's eyes.

'Wolfie has a fascinating past. I'll tell you his story sometime.' Aurora smiled fondly at him. 'Wolfie has magic of his own.' Then addressing him directly, she said, 'Wolfie, you will stay by Lia's side and make sure she comes to no harm.' Wolfie waved his tail at the sound of her voice. As an afterthought, Aurora turned to me. 'I must warn you, though, that when you walk him always take him along the beach, never into woods. He had a frightening experience a long time ago in a forest, and he has never really recovered from it.' Wolfie gave a small whine at the memory.

And so it was decided: my education in the craft and practice of magic would begin at once and Wolfie would become my constant companion. In the days that followed Aurora began intensively teaching me the ways of witchcraft. We took long morning walks together along the beach. I paddled through lacy-edged waves lapping the shore whilst Aurora explained the philosophy and principles of white magic. At night, Wolfie slept at the foot of my bed and became my shadow, guarding and protecting me.

☾

'The first thing you have to understand, Lia,' Aurora said during our first such walk, 'is that when you connect your personal power to the powers which govern the universe it must always be for the wellbeing of others. You can't go wrong if you keep these words as the rule you live by.' She quoted:

These eight words will the rede fulfil,
An' it harm none do what ye will.

'What does it mean?' I asked, stooping down to collect pretty pebbles and shells to decorate my bedroom.

'It means simply that if you live by our set of principles you will never use your magic with the intention of harming anyone. Always remember,' she wagged her finger, 'black magic is bound to backfire.'

Later back in her sun-room we warmed our cold hands by cupping them around mugs of steaming hot chocolate. She plumped the cushions and settled herself comfortably into her wooden rocking chair and, picking up her knitting, she eyed me thoughtfully.

'Of course, I cannot really teach you magic. You either have it within you or you do not. I can only teach you how to channel it and use it wisely. If you are prepared to apply yourself and study, with patience and willingness, the possibilities are endless. Your special gift is to influence and command the elements, and that can be a wonderful force for good. When you have mastered your magic, you will become a truly powerful witch.'

'When did you know you were magic, Aurora?' I asked, encouraging her to reveal more of her enchanted past to me.

'It was just something I always knew,' she said, laying her knitting aside. 'My magic was as much part of me as breathing, but then I was raised back in different times from you. Back then faerie folk and humans lived in communities side by side in harmony. We had many things in common. Faerie folk could help humans but' – she wagged her finger – 'we could also harm them. Faerie folk were respected and held in high esteem by humans because we had powers beyond that of mere mortals. We were known for our healing powers but we could also protect wells, streams, crops and fishing grounds. We worked alongside humans in their communities, just as we do now.'

'As we do now? Does that mean there are other witches living on the islands?'

'Yes! Indeed there are.' She smiled. 'Our islands still have strong pagan traditions and customs. Our ancient sites and strong connection to nature and the elements make this a fertile environment for the survival of magic. There are many witches like us, though nowadays most prefer to be known as spae-women. We have lived among human folk on those islands since ancient times, respected and revered within the community. Because we have foresight and second sight, we are trusted to use our magic to forestall the evil influence of those witches who work against the natural world.'

I leaned closer, fascinated. 'Where are these other

witches … spae-women? Are there any like me?'

Aurora eyed me with mild amusement. 'You mean, are there any young witches like you?'

Giving her a wide grin, I nodded. I was thinking how good it would be to make friends with someone like myself. Someone of my own age who understood me. Someone who had magic in them!

Aurora sensed my wistfulness. 'The answer is yes, of course, there are witches of your own age, Lia, and you will meet them. As I mentioned, I'm travelling to visit a craft fair, and many of my people will be there. I'm invited to play my fiddle. Music is an important part of our festivities.'

'Really! A craft fair. I love stalls and home bakes. I can't wait!' I jumped up, clapping my hands.

'It's not that kind of craft fair,' she said, laughing.' It's a witchcraft fare. You recall I showed you my seasonal events calendar? We are approaching Ostara, the celebration of spring. It's a particularly inspiring time when the light is growing and the sun is about to burst forth, giving us renewed energy. A very good reason to celebrate and have a party, don't you agree?'

Like all good storytellers, Aurora kept the best until last. 'If you would like to come, I'll take you with me. It'll be a great day out. There'll be feasting, dancing, music …'

'Really!' I burst out. 'You'll take me with you? Yes! I would love to come.' I hugged her.

'Good. Then that settles it.' She set her palms down on the table. 'On the twentieth of March we'll set off to Eyneholm Island at dawn. I'll make all the arrangements.

Now come on,' she coaxed.

'Let's do something fun! We can't always just be talking about magic; let's go and practise some.'

'Wow! Can we?' I followed her into the kitchen, wondering what she had in mind.

'Brrr ... it's chilly in here, isn't it.' She rubbed her hands together. 'Should we light the fire?'

'OK.' I said, eyeing her big black range. 'Should I pile on some wood?'

'Do you mean to say you don't know how to lay a fire?' she tutted. 'Well, it's time you did. Look.' She showed me. 'Firstly, screw up paper into doughnut shapes like this.' She curled paper into tight balls. 'Then lay little twigs on top like this.' She scattered the twigs liberally over the paper, now layer on the bigger sticks.' She watched as I arranged wedges of wood on top. 'Good. Now, before we put the bigger logs on, we have to light this kindling to get the fire started.'

I looked around for matches.

'No. You are going to light the fire by the power of your thought.'

'No way! How do I do that?' I looked to her for the answer.

'You have to work it out.' She folded her arms. 'You're more than capable.'

I sat staring at the logs for ages, willing them to light, but nothing happened.

Aurora met my eyes. 'You have to concentrate very hard on your intent. What is it you want to happen, Lia?'

'I want the fire to light,' I affirmed.

'Yes, but how much do you desire it?'

'I don't know what you mean? I'm trying really hard but nothing's happening.' I shrugged.

'You may be trying really hard,' she said, 'but that isn't enough!'

'But what else can I do?' I said, screwing up my face.

'You have to tap into the part of yourself that will make it happen. Visualise fire. Go on, conjure up a picture of it in your mind's eye. Now really feel its heat, smell its smoke, see its flame leap, hear it crackle. Concentrate, Lia!' her voice rose. 'THINK fire! What is your intention? What is your desire?'

I squeezed my eyes shut and concentrated fully on my task. I brought an image of leaping flames to the forefront of my mind. I heard the fire crackle. I felt its heat as I chanted my first ever spell:

It is my will and my desire
To conjure and ignite this fire!

A little flame spluttered in the grate and the fire caught! I whooped in triumph. 'I did it, Aurora! I conjured fire!'

Chapter 10

If you're thinking sorcery comes naturally to a witch, then let me tell you, you're wrong! You have to work at it. I rose from my bed at first light and crossed boggy fields and muddy ditches seeking out the botanicals required to brew my potions. I learned to avoid those plants and fungus which are deadly poisonous and must not be touched. I tore myself on tangled bushes and prickly brambles foraging for the elusive plants I needed for my spells. I saved the precious first drops of morning dew while grubbing around in the damp earth seeking out plants which grow in wild places – sorrel, chamomile, red clover, mint, mugwort, parsley, angelica, bladderwrack, gutweed and silverweed. All these were necessary to make my elixirs, and, as Aurora insisted, must be used fresh, not wilted, and the quantities measured very precisely. Before the sun had fully risen I carried my treasures back to her home.

'Come away in from the cold!' Aurora was waiting for me on her doorstep and welcomed me into her cosy kitchen. I breathed in the faint smell of lamp oil, cedarwood and lavender polish and realised how comfortable and at home I felt here. She'd been busy preparing for my lesson. Her cauldron had been scoured. Gleaming phials and glass bottles were set on the table beside her pestle and mortar.

'Choose one.' She pushed a box of coloured candles across the table to me. I chose mauve.

'Excellent choice. Mauve for wisdom.' She smiled.

'What's this copper pot out for?' I lifted the wooden spurtle lying beside it.

'For making porridge,' she laughed. 'You'll no do good work on an empty stomach.'

While she cooked us breakfast I emptied my basket of greenery onto her worktop.

'Look what I found,' I said, handing her a little bunch of delicate dark-purple flowers.

Pushing her hair back, she took the pretty posy and separating one stem she held it to her nose. 'Oh, you've been on the heath. Those flowers are very rare so you must pick them very sparingly. They're a species only found on our islands. Primula orcadia. Well done for hunting them out … And what else have you brought me? Eyebright. Just what I needed. Thrift, and oh you've found some early spring quill, good lass.'

Having plumped the cushions on her big armchair, I sank into its soft warmth and stretched out my legs, kicking off my shoes and toasting my toes at the fire.

'Here you are, lass.' She lowered a tray onto my knees.

I hungrily ate the bowl of creamy porridge drizzled with honey and afterwards felt completely full and contented.

'You spoil me, Aurora. That was so yummy!'

'I like to see you tucking in. Here. There's a wee spot left.'

She scraped the last of the porridge into my bowl. After I'd washed out the pot, she placed her palms flat on the table.

'Now then. If you're ready, let's begin.'

I took a seat beside her giving her my full attention.

'You've already had some experience of using your magic.' Her eyes gave me a knowing look, but I'm supposing only as a spontaneous unplanned gut-response to an event?'

'Yes. That's right.' I blinked.

She placed her hand over mine. 'I want to tutor you in the art and craft of magic. I can teach you how to take control of your power, but we should begin with something simple.' She pressed her fingers to her lips, as she mulled the matter over. As she flicked through the pages of her spell book she muttered, 'Hmmm. Drawing an item to you. Repelling it. No ...' She turned the page. 'Too easy ...' Licking her finger to turn the pages more quickly, she paused and bookmarked a chapter. Rubbing her hands together, she finally exclaimed, 'Yes! This should be perfect ... But before we attempt to create the spell I think it could be helpful and sensible to study a little of the theory of magic.' Touching the leg of her spectacles, she gave me a solemn look. 'The very first thing you should understand, Lia, is this. The universe is filled with energy. Casting a spell is simply harnessing that energy. I'm aware you felt more than a little frightened when your powers began to surface.' She rolled her eyes. 'I'm not surprised. There are so many frightening myths about witches, but if you want to know the truth you can be a witch and still be yourself.'

I sneaked a look at her under my lashes. 'How do

you mean?'

'I mean in real life a witch is simply someone aware of her power who can put that power into action. Someone who has learned to raise and direct energy.' Her forehead puckered. 'You see magic in itself isn't good or bad, black or white. It is how you use it. Be very aware, if you perform magic to harm someone, that harm will come back to harm you threefold.' She leaned back in her chair.

'My best advice to you, Lia, would be this.' She steepled her fingers. 'Always work with the universe, never against it.'

Under her watchful eyes, I attempted to perform my first simple spell of transfiguration.

She placed a piece of wood bark on the table and asked me to grate it. 'I want you to do this all by yourself,' she insisted. 'That is the way you'll learn.'

She swapped places with me and placed the open spell book before me, pointing to the page heading:

Transfiguration
This spell is used to vanish both animated and inanimate objects into 'non-being.'

Next, she placed an egg on the table and lit the mauve candle.

'Just follow the instructions exactly.' She kept her eye on my every move, commenting on my efforts with a mere 'mmmm, yes good!' and a slight nod or a 'tut-tut!' and a slight shake of her head.

Carefully gathering my elements together I ran my finger down the list. 'Ach, I'm short of one ingredient,' I groaned. 'Do you have any dried kelp in your kitchen store cupboard, Aurora?'

She adjusted her specs and fixed me with a disapproving stare. 'Herbs and plants are a living conduit to the Earth's energy and interact with the elements. The earth nurtures them, water feeds their growth, the sun makes them thrive, the wind scatters their seeds.' She waggled a finger at me, 'You must use them freshly picked, NEVER dried. You must be very particular in this, Lia. Their vital energy must not be compromised.'

In that first lesson, of course, all I brewed were mistakes.

Aurora pinched the bridge of her nose. 'Too much thistledown, not enough verbena, far too much cobweb, and tut, you forgot to add the dandelion leaf.' She checked everything and didn't let me get away with anything. She taught me that spell making is not only about what you add to the mix. You have to pay attention to how you chop it, the exact quantities you add, the way you chant over it. There's a very specialised skill to be learned. You have to feel where the power gathers and speak the right words to draw it to its height.

I became disheartened. Even after taking the greatest care gathering my ingredients and chanting my words to perfection, my spells failed. On the second week of my lessons, with Aurora's ever-watchful eyes on me, I gathered together all my elements with the intention of making a spell of transmutation – in this instance, to change a gull's feather into a white dove. It wasn't going well.

'I don't know why it doesn't work for me,' I groaned, slumping my shoulders.

'I'm taking care to measure my ingredients exactly. I'm using the correct chants. Where am I going wrong?' I knitted my eyebrows in a sulky frown while emptying the cauldron of unproductive smelly green slime out of the window.

Aurora held up her finger. 'Have you no' been listening tae anything I've said, lass?' It's no' just about putting together the correct ingredients and saying the right words. You have to feel your intention.'

'You always say that to me but what do you mean by intention?' I set the empty cauldron back on the stovetop in a huff.

She let out a frustrated hmmmph ... 'All right. Let's go over it once again, Lia.' She counted off on her fingers. 'Firstly, you have to couple all that you've learned with your intention. Second, summon up your magic. Third, bring it to the forefront of your thoughts. Fourth, clear your mind of everything else. Fifth, visualise your intended outcome and sixth, and perhaps above all ...' – she fastened her eyes on mine – 'believe you can do it!'

I slouched against the wall, wrinkling my nose. 'But I thought that's what I was doing.'

Adopting a schoolmarm tone, Aurora began to lecture me: 'Developing your magic is like developing a muscle. The more you use it, the stronger it will become.'

Picking at a rag-nail I blurted out, 'I don't think I can do it. Maybe I don't have what it takes.'

79

She touched my arm. 'Look. I know I sounded harsh but it's because I don't want you to give up!' She squeezed my shoulder. 'You need to work on your scepticism and resistance.'

She rapped out a drumroll on the table. 'Come on! Less of this self-doubt. Try, try, try again.

'OK!' I gave a long sigh.' I'll give it one last try but if it doesn't work this time I'm quitting.'

Following exactly as she advised, I cleared my mind of everything except the gull's feather. I chopped and blended my ingredients meticulously. I closed my eyes and envisaged a beautiful white dove materialise. I visualised it for the longest time in my mind's eye. I chanted my words three times over:

Feather of gull take wing and fly,
Once more you'll soar high in the sky.

I opened my eyes and stared at the feather … Nothing!

'I'm done,' I said, close to tears. Reaching for my hoodie, I mumbled in a petulant tone, 'This isn't working. I'm going home.'

Aurora placed her hand lightly on my shoulder to delay me leaving.

'Nae need for you to go in the poots, Lia. Look.'

The feather was gone. A white dove perched a moment on the windowsill before flying off into the twilight.

'Well done! You see. You can do it.'

Giving a broad grin, I punched the air! Yes! I felt fantastic.

My enthusiasm was back and my self-confidence restored.

'That was epic! Can we do some more magic? Pleeeease!'

'Golly no.' She started to clear the table. 'It'll be dark soon. She massaged the back of her neck. 'It's been a busy day. Performing magic takes it out of you. I'm fair puggled.'

She flopped into her armchair and suggested I stay over. 'Since we have to leave early tomorrow for the fair and it's such a filthy night, you should phone your mum to say you'll sleep-over here tonight? She has to leave early tomorrow, too. It makes sense.'

'No.' I shook my head. 'Thanks anyway but I have to go home.' I described my new designer-label jeans and trainers to her. 'Mum sent over the Firth for them. When I meet them all tomorrow for the first time I want to be wearing them.'

'Okie-dokie!' Her eyes twinkled. 'I have to confess I'm no' much up on the current fashions.' She brushed her hand over her baggy green jumper! Glancing at the clock she drew in a sharp breath. 'Michty. It'll be dark soon. It's high time you made your way home. Let me get my coat I'll walk doon with you, Lia.'

'No. Don't come out. You're tired and it's a horrible night. Don't worry. I'll be fine. I have Wolfie with me.'

'Weel, all right, if you're sure, but' – she tapped her fingers on the table – 'no dawdling, mind, and remember to come up here early tomorrow morning. We have to leave for Eynenholm at first light.

'I will. I'm so excited! I can't wait!' I bounced up and down on my toes. 'I don't think I'll be able to sleep tonight.'

'Well, try! We have a big day tomorrow. Wrapping

81

her arms around me, she gave me an unexpected hug and standing back leaving her hands resting on my shoulders she praised me. 'You did well today, Lia. You can feel proud of yourself!'

'Thank you, Aurora.' I beamed.

'Here. Tak my big coat. It's no' a night tae be worrying aboot fashion.'

She helped me into the tent-like coat, buttoning me into it.

'Bye. See you first thing tomorrow!' I called, closing her front door behind me.

Chapter 11

Stepping out into the half-light, I hunched down against the foul weather feeling glad of Aurora's coat's protection. I pulled my collar up around my face, muffling myself against the damp murky mist swirling around me and headed down to the shore, realising with slight unease that, apart from having Wolfie with me, I was out alone. Not another soul had braved this filthy night. A slow feeling of apprehension began to creep over me. Soon the dusk would turn to dark. I should get home as quickly as possible. It would make sense to take the short cut along the seaside path. The warm yellow lights of our cottage were just visible in the distance.

I hurried homewards, quickening my pace and keeping my head down, I shielded my face from the stinging sand that was tossed up by blusters of gusty wind. A thick clammy fog wrapped itself around us, obscuring the path. I shivered, wishing I had heeded Aurora's advice and stayed put. I could hardly see a thing. Wolfie's grey outline drifted in and out of swirling pockets of claggy mist.

'Please stay close to me, Wolfie,' I said and heard a tremor of fear in my voice.

I extended my arm in front of me and let out a little sigh of relief when he pushed his cold wet nose into my

83

hand. Wolfie fell into step with me, and I kept hold of his ruff to reassure myself that he was close.

As the path wound nearer to the beach, I became aware of a putrid stench hanging thick in the air. Sometimes you get that from the rotting carcass of a beached sea-animal, a seal, perhaps, or once, Aurora told me to my wide-eyed astonishment, a whale. No. It couldn't be that. Aurora knows everything that happens on the island. She would have told me if there had been another beached sea-creature. The stink became stronger as the path wound closer to the sea, giving me the jitters. My intuition, my sixth sense, warned me to turn back. A disquieting feeling someone or something was watching me gripped me. My eyes darted all around, and breathing hard I broke into a run, tripping and stumbling over ruts and stones in my desperate hurry to get home. Suddenly, Wolfie gave a deep rumbling growl.

'Wolfie, what's wrong? You're frightening me.' I clutched his ruff, feeling his hackles rise.

Tracking his gaze, the silvery moon's glow over the water illuminated something that completely unnerved me. Something sinister and unearthly taking shape out in the bay.

Wolfie sat quivering, fixing his eyes on the apparition. I strained my eyes in the half-light to properly make out the dark shadowy form in the water which was now visibly moving shoreward in the murky fog. At first, I couldn't be sure if it was a trick of the light but then I saw it clearly. Two red glowing eyes appeared above the water's surface hanging suspended there, scanning the shoreline.

'What is that?' I whispered, staring out to where the sea shifted and parted. The shadowy creature snaked through the water towards the shallows, its red glowing eyes focused on us. I gaped in horror as it gave a great thunderous snort and thrashed through the waves, surfacing so close to me I could now see its hideous form clearly. The creature had the torso of a man and the body of a horse, like a centaur but with flap-like fins growing from its legs. Its entire hairless and skinless body looked like raw living flesh, its transparent veins pumped black blood. A gasp escaped me as the grotesque beast propelled itself powerfully through the surf towards us, roaring and exhaling putrid vapour. It fixed me with its blazing eyes and it illuminated me in a blood-red beam.

Wolfie frantically ran back and forth on the shoreline, snarling and growling, snapping and barking at the threatening monster.

Run! I thought but my legs wouldn't obey; they were paralysed by fear.

'Wolfie! Do something!' I sobbed in panic.

Wolfie stood stock-still, his eyes narrowing and fixing me in a mesmerising stare. Then by some charm, hex, spell or magic, call it what you will, he spoke to me. No, I don't mean in a human way. He communicated through a meeting of our minds. Honestly, I felt so terrified I didn't stop to question it.

'Listen to me carefully, Lia, and do exactly as I tell you,' he counselled. 'Tyra has unleashed the Nuckelavee. It is the cruellest, wickedest and most savage of her creatures. She has charged it with destroying you. You must act swiftly.'

'What can I do?' I wailed, petrified.

He stood staring at me his amber eyes glowing.

'There's no time to run! You have to summon magic to see it off!'

'But I don't think I have powerful enough magic to stop it.' I wavered.

Wolfie barked back: 'It can be stopped by your magic if you act now. It has a fatal weakness. It cannot cross fresh water.'

'What do you mean?' I stammered.

He let out a single harsh howl: 'Use your power to summon rain!'

'But I can't. I don't know how to,' I whimpered.

Wolfie drew his lips back in a snarl. 'Lia, now is not the time to doubt yourself! You have to trust in your abilities. You are a powerful witch. If you believe in yourself, you can do anything. Tap into the part of yourself that will turn your desire into reality. Do it. NOW!'

'Concentrate!' I scolded myself, gathering my wits together. 'You can do this! Drawing in a deep breath to calm myself and stilling my mind and body, I reached deep down into the part of myself where my magic lives. Clenching my fists, I dug my nails into my palms and focused all of my will into unlocking my energy. I squeezed my eyes closed and concentrated my entire being on bringing my magic to the fore. Aurora's words filtered through the clamour in my head.

'What is your intention?'

I centred my thoughts on visualising dark rain clouds scudding across the sky. I willed them to come to my aid. The atmosphere became electrified. The sky became blanketed, layer upon layer, in thick grey raincloud.

'What is your desire?'

87

Holding my arms up to the leaden skies, I unleashed my magic. I commanded the elements:

Bring forth a mighty deluge of rain!

At once, the heavens opened and heavy torrents of rain began falling in sheets. The monstrous beast bellowed its rage into the night and spinning around it disappeared, plunging under the waves in a great spume of sea-spray. Hardly daring to breathe, I clutched at my chest and collapsed onto the wet sand, suddenly feeling weak and faint. I sat there hugging my arms around myself taking in deep gulping breaths. Wolfie stood stiffly, tail up, ears up, his eyes anchored on the water, alert for any further disturbance. I pushed myself up onto shaky legs and ran a trembling hand along his back.

'Is it over, Wolfie? Are we safe?'

As soon as my legs felt steadier and my heart stopped hammering, I took to my heels and we ran for home.

'Lia! Is that you?" Mum came through to the kitchen in her dressing gown. 'I heard you come in. I've been worried about you. What happened to you? Aurora said you left ages ago.'

There was no way I could answer her questions. I couldn't put into words what had just taken place.

'I'm OK, Mum. I had to shelter from the downpour,' I lied.

'Poor you!' she sympathised. 'Come here, darlin'. You're completely soaked through.' She fussed around me helping me out of my sodden clothes. Giving me a concerned look, she quizzed, 'Do you feel all right, pet? You're shaking.'

No way did I want to worry her before she left me with Aurora to go to Edinburgh to do her TV Interview. It would be better if I confided everything to Aurora in the morning. She would help me. Besides, I needed time to think. This had changed everything. I had grave doubts now about putting myself into danger by crossing over into the realms of magic.

$* \maltese * \maltese *$

'I'm OK, Mum, just cold and wet,' I answered through chattering teeth.

She towel-dried my hair and felt my brow.

'I hope you're not coming down with something.'

'Mum. I've said I'm OK.' I snatched my pyjamas from her. 'I'm going to bed now.'

She shrugged. 'All right. No need to be so crabbit with me!'

'Sorry,' I apologised. 'I know it's a big day for you tomorrow.' I spoke in a chummier tone. 'What time are you leaving in the morning?'

She replied in an anxious voice. 'Early. Straight after you go up to Aurora's. I'm nervous. I'm so new to this job and they ask me to go to Edinburgh to do a TV interview. I've never appeared on TV before.' She twisted her hair around her finger, her habit when she's worried.

'But I've got to do this. It should raise awareness about our conservation project and get us funding.' Her brow creased. 'I'm not looking forward to the journey, though. You know how terrified I am of flying.'

'I know. I'm the same. I'm scared of flying, too,' I said sympathetically.

Mum blinked. 'Aside from the carbon footprint issue, the plane's an old bone-shaker! It's meant to take light cargo, not people.' She chewed her nail. 'I wish I was going by car and ferry but the short notice gives me no option. Anyway. It's late, pet. Let's try to get some sleep.'

The sheets tangled around me as I lay in bed. I was restless, the pumping adrenalin preventing sleep from coming. I punched the pillows to plump them and got up to make sure my windows were securely and tightly shut. Feeling my way back to bed, I tripped over Wolfie.

'Sorry!' I stretched my hand down to him. 'Are you asleep?' I whispered.

'Nope,' he yawned. 'I'm wide awake.'

'Wow! We really can communicate!' I leaned over the side of the bed, gawking at him. 'This is bonkers!'

'Not really,' he replied in a matter-of-fact tone. 'In the world of magic anything can happen. You and I can communicate telepathically. But you understand, Lia, it's only people with magical abilities who can hear me.'

'You have a Scottish accent,' I whispered into the dark.

'Aye.' His voice was tinged with pride. 'Born and raised in Scotland, or Caledonia as it was known back in

those days.'

This intrigued me, 'Back in which days, Wolfie?'

'Back in 1645,' he answered.

'Really! You're actually centuries old? Tell me your story, Wolfie. Please!'

His eyes glinted amber in the dark. 'In my early years, I roamed freely with my pack in the wilds of the Scottish Highlands. Tragically, our settled way of life was violently disrupted when our habitat became the scene of a mighty battle.'

Now I was wide awake. 'What happened to you?'

'The pack fled deep into the safety of the Great Wood, the ancient Forest of Caledon. I somehow became separated from them.' I heard the catch in his voice. 'That was when I became a lone wolf.'

'And that's when you became Aurora's wolf?' I delved.

'That is a long story for another time.' He lay down, sighing into his paws. 'Let's try to get some sleep now.'

Chapter 12

Don't you often find if you have a difficult choice to make the solution comes to you after you sleep on it? I couldn't shake off my feelings of dread from my encounter with the sea- monster. After a night of tossing and turning, I concluded I was way out of my depth. I made up my mind the minute I got up I'd had enough of dabbling in magic. I wanted nothing more to do with witchcraft. It wasn't safe.

'Mum, are you awake?' I padded into her room and perched on the edge of her bed.

'Yeah,' she mumbled in a sleep-heavy voice. 'What's wrong? Have we slept in?' Checking her phone her eyes snapped open. 'Oh, pants! We have.' She swung her legs over the side of the bed.

'Lia, can you get yourself breakfast? I have to be at the airfield for 9 a.m.'

'Yeah, fine. I'll let you have your shower first.'

Speaking through a mouthful of toothpaste, she mumbled, 'Thanks, darlin'. Shouldn't you be making tracks for Aurora's house? She's expecting you up there early, isn't she?

It just blurted out.

'I don't want to go, Mum. Couldn't I stay home today?'

'Eh? Lia, what's wrong, pet? What's happened to

change your mind? Yesterday you couldn't wait to go to Eynenholm with Aurora! ... Come here.' She sat back down patting the bed. 'Sit here beside me. Talk to me.'

'Nothing's happened.' I cuddled into her. 'It's just I've decided to stop my magic lessons.'

She lifted surprised eyebrows. 'Tell me. What's happened to make you change your mind? Ach. Are you just being fickle?'

'Mum, I need you to listen to me. I've decided I want to be like you, human. I'm going to let go of my magic. I want it to wither.' Holding my palms up to her, I said forcefully, 'And you can't make me change my mind. I'm having nothing more to do with witchcraft.' My lower lip trembled. 'I'm finished with it!'

'Och what on earth's brought this on? Alright. Don't get upset,' she said, stroking my hair. 'It has to be your own choice, and whatever you decide you know I'll support you. Aurora will understand, too, so stop worrying.'

She took two dresses out of the wardrobe and eyed them puckering her brow. 'You should go up and tell her now, though, but I think it'll disappoint her, Lia.' She rubbed at a stain on the collar of the red dress. 'Make-up,' she tutted. Fiddling with her earring, she said, 'You know, you should go to Eynenholm with Aurora today. I used to go to those festivals.' Her eyes lit up. 'You'll enjoy yourself. It'll be a fun day. Besides, I'm going to be away till late tonight. I can't leave you here on your own, can I?'

'Take me with you.' I clasped my hands, pleading with her.

Concern flickered in her eyes. 'What's all this about? I can't take you, Lia. There are no spare seats on the plane.' She held her palm up. 'That's all there is to it.'

Hopping on one foot, she stepped into the blue dress.

'Zip me up, can you? Thanks Li. I hope it's a calm day for flying,' she burbled on. 'Not too windy.' Anxiety was evident in her voice. 'I don't like flying, especially not on vintage planes! Oh jings.' She placed her hand on her stomach. 'Butterflies. I've never been on telly before. Put the kettle on, there's a good lass. I have to have another look at my notes.'

I could see she had more than enough on her mind without me adding to her worries.

'OK,' I sighed. 'I'll go. I'll spend the day with Aurora.'

'Awe, you're a good kid,' she muttered, taking a slurp of tea and sticking her nose into her notes.

While I dried my hair I rehearsed the speech I would make to Aurora. I would politely but firmly insist that a life of witchcraft was definitely not for me.

'I'm going up to Aurora's now.' I leaned over Mum and ruffled her hair.

'Bye, darlin'.' She gave me a distracted air-kiss. 'Hope your day goes well, Mum,' I called out as an afterthought.

She barely looked up from her notes. 'Mmmm … have fun, pet. See you later.'

Wolfie fell into step with me as I trudged along the rain slicked seaside road to Aurora's house. I convinced myself I was doing the right thing. I would tell Aurora everything. I would talk to her about the terrifying event of the previous night. That would explain my feelings. I would tell her I had made a decision. A life of magic and witchcraft was definitely not for me. As Wolfie and I approached her home, a sense of unease crept over me. I recognised that feeling. My sixth sense niggled at me.

Something's not right. Her front door had been left open. That's unusual, I thought, stepping into the porch calling out her name. Aurora didn't answer.

The hair on the back of my neck prickled. Something's definitely wrong. I took a tentative step into her hall while holding on to Wolfie's ruff. 'Aurora!' I called her name again, venturing further in.

First, I looked into her bedroom. Empty. Her bed hadn't been slept in. The house felt creepy. I pushed the sun-room door open. Empty. I warily poked my head around the kitchen door. 'Woooah! What on earth's happened in here?' I said in a shaky voice. Wolfie pushed past me into the kitchen.

'Looks like the house has been ransacked,' I whispered, 'and Aurora's gone.'

Aurora's kitchen looked like a battle zone. Broken phials of fermented yellow liquid spilt everywhere. A compass and four black feathers lay in a puddle of murky brown stuff on the rug. Aurora's music sheets had been scattered, her chairs upturned, her drawers pulled out, their contents emptied and strewn over the floor. Most worrying of all she hadn't taken her fiddle. I found it propped up in the corner, proving without doubt that for whatever reason she must have had to leave in a huge hurry.

'She wouldn't have gone to the Ostara celebrations without taking it. She's been rehearsing her music for ages. She was looking forward to playing it at the gathering. I raked a hand through my hair. 'I can't understand this. She wouldn't have gone without me.'

'Or me.' Wolfie's eyes drooped. 'What is that smell?' He sniffed the air.

A pungent odour seeped from a resinous green murky liquid fermenting in a cauldron on the stove. Wolfie sniffed it and padded around curious items laid out on the kitchen floor. A clock, a silver charm, four black feathers, a map and a crystal were placed at the points of a drawn-out pentacle. Aurora's spell book lay open beside them.

'I think I can piece together what's happened here,' he said, grimacing. 'Aurora's been preparing a complicated spell for travel. Of course,' his nostrils flared, his distaste obvious; 'she has a broomstick but it's a stubborn, thrawn thing. In my opinion, she should have thrown it on to the bonfire years ago. Huh!' His tone became scathing, 'The besom thinks it's indispensable but it isn't! Oh! If I had my way …'

I interrupted his tirade.

'Do you mean she was experimenting with a new kind of spell for our travel to Eynenholm Island?'

He nodded. 'Nowadays you see, with new wisdom and the correct spell it's possible to harness the earth's energy. You simply transpose yourself from one place to another in the blink of an eye.' He scowled. 'In a way, this is your fault!'

I burst out indignantly 'What! How can you blame me for her disappearance?'

'Don't get uppity with me.' His eyes sparked. 'I only meant Aurora worried that her magic had become outdated. She wanted to impress you, Lia, by showing you she could use new modern ways to cast a spell for instant travel. I warned her against such vanity but she wouldn't be told. She was stubbornly determined to experiment with new ways.'

'And you suspect this experiment has gone badly wrong for her?'

He exhaled a long breath. 'Magic is very potent and must be treated with the greatest care and respect. I'm afraid her attempts at trying the new ways have not been well judged. Last year she attempted to evoke a spell for instant travel to take us to Blackpool. It took us weeks to clean up the slimy pool of black water in the garden.' He shook his head at the memory.' She's been at it again! She's probably got her magic quite muddled, and that' – his eyes narrowed – 'would make her wide open to the possibility of mishap.'

'Do you mean she's put herself in danger?' I asked, alarmed.

A muscle in Wolfie's jaw twitched. 'She's opened herself up to the possibility of being overcome by dark magic.'

'You mean she's left herself vulnerable to Tyra's ambush. If you're right,' I said, 'what can we do?'
He paced the kitchen floor. 'She may have triggered a spell which pitched her plans into chaos. Best-case scenario she's arrived at Eynenholm Island a wee tad early.'

'But what if she hasn't arrived at all?' I watched closely for his reaction.

His eyes grew serious. 'If that is the case, then I suspect the worst.'

'The worst?' I shot him a look.

'Tyra has long awaited a chance to take control. By seizing Aurora, she gains the upper hand.'

I felt the blood drain from my face. 'We have to leave for Eynenholm Island right away, Wolfie. We've got to know if she's safe.'

'Slow down, Lia.' he said in a stern tone. 'Yes. I'm going after her but I can't take you with me.' He shook his head. 'It's too risky. You're still very inexperienced. A mere novice. You've still too much to learn.'

'But I've been making good progress. Aurora said so,' I protested.

He blew out his cheeks. 'This quest could lead into extremely dangerous territory.'

'I'm not afraid!' I eyed him boldly. 'You have no right to stop me. Now when do we leave?'

'I said no.' He glared. 'I'm going alone. Taking you into the heart of Tyra's domain would put both of us in danger. Besides,' he glowered, 'I thought you had finished with magic?'

'Yes, that was true earlier this morning but not now!' I flashed an angry look at him. 'Tyra thought by sending her sea-monster she would frighten me into running away.' I clenched my fists. 'Well …' – I raised my chin – 'I almost did run, but she's crossed a line. Her threats to my family have made me realise we'll never be safe until she's stopped! I'm quite certain of the path I'm taking now, Wolfie. I'm going to become the strongest most powerful witch of all. I'm going to fight her and I will win.'

Wolfie's forehead furrowed. 'Are you quite sure you're prepared for whatever may come?'

'Yes. I'm sure, except for just one thing,' I hesitated. 'I can't go missing, too. I can't do that to Mum.'

Wolfie's intelligent eyes met mine. 'I know of a way we can go and not be missed.'

'Perfect,' I said. 'But how do we do that?'

'Teleportation,' he replied. 'We evoke a spell to make time cease to flow for everyone except us. It will enable us to travel through time portals into different dimensions without being missed or detected. We'll arrive back only a second or a fraction of a second after we've left. No one will know we've been away.

I clapped my hands. 'Wolfie. You're the best! How soon can you conjure the spell for our travel?'

'Not so hasty, Lia,' he replied. 'Remember these things can't be rushed. You must be aware that spells, like knives, can be used for good and bad. Summoning the gods and spirits lightly could have dire consequences. You have to be careful what you ask for and plan everything meticulously. My magic isn't strong enough to conjure this spell so you will do it!'

'Me? No way! You think I can conjure a spell to make time stand still! Even if I could I don't know the way to Eynenholm Island. How can I get us there if I don't know where it is?'

He groaned. 'By magic, of course, but dearie me, you're doubting yourself already.'

He glanced up at the ceiling muttering, 'I don't know if this is the right decision. Taking you with me makes us both vulnerable. I can guide you but you have to make it happen. You've already shown you have powerful inner magic, but you have to believe in yourself to strengthen it. You're still very much a beginner, Lia..."

'I'm a fast learner!' I butted in.

'Yes, you're learning but' – he eyed me sceptically – 'you still have to learn to have faith in yourself. Open yourself to it completely.'

'No more arguments, Wolfie. I'm coming with you! I know I can do this.' I hugged him around the neck. 'Trust me. I won't let you down, I promise!'

He paused considering a moment. 'All right. If you're certain sure of this, then I'll be glad of your help. I only hope I don't regret this decision.'

'You won't! Come on, Wolfie. Let's make a start.'

His expression grew serious. 'Very well, let's do this. First, you have to go outside to the garden and find yourself a quiet place to sit and meditate.'

'What does that mean?' I asked.

'It just means you reflect deeply,' he explained. 'Ask Mother Earth to determine our fate. Clear all thoughts from your mind and allow yourself to be open and receptive to her counsel.'

I immediately set about my task. I chose a wooden bench tucked away in a sheltered, secluded corner of Aurora's garden and composing myself sat perfectly still. Closing my eyes, I emptied my mind of all thoughts and drifted into that half-conscious state you go into before sleep comes. From that moment I had no control over my thoughts and actions. I lost all awareness of time and became oblivious to my surroundings. An external force took control. It began to communicate instructions to me:

*Botanicals must be gathered under a
dark moon -
during the fifth minute of the fifth hour,
a red-haired maiden wearing a red
gown should pick twelve red berries from
a holly bush. Place one berry on each of
the sundial's markings. Drink three drops
ONLY from the potion in the cauldron.
Process this very precisely. The first three
drops will convey wisdom, insight and
success to your purpose - any more will be
deadly poisonous.*

A chill in the air brought me back to consciousness with
a shiver. I have no idea how long I'd spent outside in this
trance-like state, but some hours must have passed because
when I awoke the sun had dropped low in the sky. Back in
the house, Wolfie waited patiently.

'I've done it, Wolfie. I have a spell to stop time.
That's our first problem solved but how are we going to
travel?'

'Follow me.' Wolfie beckoned. 'I have something to
show you.'

Chapter 13

He led the way through Aurora's hall to a door hidden behind a heavy tapestry curtain. It concealed a rickety staircase leading up to a musty attic. Weak light filtering through a grime-filmed skylight window cast the attic into an eerie greenish gloom. I moved cautiously into the cramped space and stood with my mouth gaping. The attic was filled with Aurora's past. I ran my fingers over dust-covered artefacts as I moved from one curiosity to the next. A penny-farthing bicycle stood propped against a huge dark wooden wardrobe. I wondered whether Aurora would ever let me borrow that – it would be such a blast to ride it down the High Street. Aurora had collected an amazing hodgepodge of stuff – parasols, umbrellas, fire screens, warming pans, toasting forks, leather-bound books piled up in corners, albums of faded sepia photos … I lifted a dust cover from a piano and sat down to play, wondering at its unusual double keyboard. I playing a few twanging chords and stopped, complaining to Wolfie

'This piano badly needs tuning, doesn't it?'

'It isn't a piano!' Wolfe scoffed. 'It's a harpsichord. It doesn't strike the notes, it plucks them. Well, fancy that.' The corners of his eyes crinkled. 'How remarkable. It still plays perfectly despite its great age.'

'How old is it? How did Aurora come to have it,

Wolfie?' I twirled myself around on the piano stool to face him.'

His eyes narrowed. 'Let me see. It must be almost three hundred years old. My namesake gifted it to her. Hah!' He noticed my sceptical look. 'You thought Aurora named me Wolfie because I'm a wolf, didn't you? Most people think that, but no.' He eyed me with amusement.

'She named me after her great friend Wolfgang Amadeus …'

'… Mozart?' I completed his sentence, my jaw dropping. 'No way!'

'Och!' He gave me a modest look. 'There are so many tales to tell, but not now. Wheesht! We don't have time to waste.'

He sniffed around the heavy solid wardrobe. 'Do you think you could move this armoire, Lia?'

A daunting task. I thought it would be hard to shift but I had to show willing. I remembered my promise to Wolfie. I wasn't about to give up at the first hurdle. I don't know where I found the superhuman strength to shift it. Grunting and puffing, I put all my body strength behind its considerable weight and shoved it, inch by inch, away from the wall.

'There's a padlocked cupboard concealed behind it,' I said, surprised.

Wolfie jerked his head to indicate a key hanging on a hook on the wall just as a loud insistent battering noise started up against the inside of the cupboard. Something or someone behind the door wanted out!

'Take the key and open the door, Lia.' Wolfie's voice became a low growl. 'Then I warn you: stand well back!'

My hand shook as I turned the key, and as I threw the door open I leapt back. Quick as a flash, a broomstick flew out. It circled madly around the ceiling, making thrusting, darting movements at us. I backed away to a safe distance and peeped out from behind a tapestry screen.

Curling his lip, Wolfie barked an order at the broomstick: 'Desist!'

The broomstick hovered agitatedly above us whilst Wolfie paced up and down then, in a forceful voice and lapsing into a strong Scottish dialect I had difficulty understanding he barked.

'I'll tak nae mare o' yer confounded impudence, ye accursed wretch!' The broomstick spiralled down a little but hovered just out of reach.

Wolfie snarled menacingly. 'Enough of yer foolish capers! Yer disobedience offends me greatly. Osean!' The broomstick hesitated a moment before flying down to us.

'What did you say to it? What language is that, Wolfie?' I asked in a quavering voice flattening myself against the wall.

'I ordered it to obey!' Wolfie replied in a strained voice. 'When the besom exasperates me I lapse into the old Scottish Lallans tongue.' Ignoring the broomstick's buzzing noises, he turned to me. 'Lia, do you think you can master riding it?'

'What!' My eyes came out on stalks. 'Do you mean we'll be travelling on this broomstick to Eynenholm Island? Surely it's much too dangerous! I'm … I'm afraid of … of … heights,' I stuttered. 'I have a fear of flying! I could fall off!' I folded my arms and shook my head vigorously. 'No, you can't ask me to do this.'

Wolfie turned his attention back to the broomstick

and barked, 'I will say this only once, ye thrawn creature. If ye disrespect this fine lady, I will put a torch to ye and fling ye on the fire.'

At that the broomstick flew down and hovered by my feet, waiting.

How hard could this be? I persuaded myself to give it a try. I tentatively mounted it and gripped on tight … Wooooah! It reared up and bucked madly around the room then, stopping abruptly, it threw me off in mid-flight. Finally, making small swaying movements, it sashayed off, staying just out of reach. This infuriated Wolfie. He sprang at the broomstick. It deftly outflanked his snapping jaws.

'Stop, Wolfie,' I pleaded. 'Let me try again.' I rubbed my grazed elbow while speaking to the broomstick in soft persuasive words of reassurance. Taking small slow steps I approached it from the side, making no sudden moves. Careful not to startle it I grasped it firmly while continuing to speak in a gentle coaxing tone.

'Easy now. Trust me,' I crooned. 'I mean you no harm. Please help us. Your mistress has gone missing. She may be in danger. We need you to take us on a journey to search for her.' With that, the broomstick obediently floated gently down, coming to rest at my feet. Relieved it was willing to cooperate, I recalled the words of the spell: 'A maiden wearing a red dress ...'

'If I'm going to do this, I should be wearing a red dress to make the spell complete, but I don't have one,' I fretted.

Wolfie padded over to an old battered wooden chest.

'Look in here, Lia. Aurora's kept some gowns from her youth.'

Opening it raised clouds of dust and sent me into

107

a sneezing fit. Inside, I found a wonderful mish-mash of things from my granny's past: strings of jet beads and pearls, jewelled bracelets and bangles, feathered headbands and boas, fans, silk purses. 'Look at this!' I pulled out a fox-fur wrap but felt immediately sorry I had because it made Wolfie shudder. I delved down and came across a long crimson silk dress with a hooped skirt which had been carefully folded in tissue paper and tucked away at the foot of the chest.

'That will do perfectly, won't it?' Wolfie's eyes took on a faraway look. 'I remember Aurora wearing it to a concert in the Albert Hall hosted by Queen Victoria.'

'It may have been fit to wear before a queen but it's old now and it smells fusty.' I held it up in front of me, wrinkling my nose. 'All right,' I agreed. 'I suppose I'll wear it if I have to.' I stepped into the Victorian ball gown and checking myself in a long cheval mirror I couldn't help giggling. 'I look like one of the ugly sisters in Cinderella.' I said, picking up the skirts of the dress. I picked out a fan and curtseyed into the mirror. 'Your Majesty, the slipper fits. I pointed down and wiggled my baseball boot.

Wolfie ignored my silliness and reminded me in a gruff voice 'It's almost five o'clock. The blue hour. You must collect the twelve red berries and place them exactly on the points of the sundial. After you've drunk the magic elixir we can be on our way.'

'I don't really have to drink three drops of that awful goo, do I?'

'Lia.' He became deadly serious. 'We've no time to waste. If you do not drink it soon, the spell will not work.'

Without wasting any further time I picked up my red silk skirts and carefully descended the attic stairs. I did exactly as asked and searching the garden I picked twelve red berries from a holly bush. I placed them precisely where I had been instructed to on the face of Aurora's sundial. Back in the kitchen, I measured out exactly three drops of the disgusting green liquid. I held my nose and swallowed it down. Its bitter, revolting taste made me gag slightly.

'The sun is setting. It's time we set off.' Wolfie declared. 'Wear Aurora's big coat. We're heading north. It will be cold.' He straddled the broomstick with ease. I could tell he'd done it many times before. He balanced perfectly. I felt super-scared but took a deep breath and climbed on behind him. Gripping the broomstick I gritted my teeth readying myself for take-off.

Falbh Agus Itealaich!

Wolfie commanded.

'What does that mean?' I breathed, keeping my eyes scrunched tightly shut.

'Lift your wings in flight,' he replied.

'Wait! Wolfie! Won't we need to take food and water?'

'Och no,' Wolfie replied in his gruff voice. 'We're travelling to a parallel universe remember? Different rules apply. Although you may feel we've been away for a long time, the actual time that passes on Earth will only be seconds. We'll be back an instant after we leave.'

'Wait.' I dug my heels into the floor.

'What now?' he huffed. 'Any more delay could

upset the equilibrium and elements of the spell.' I grabbed the spell book and stuffed it into a satchel throwing it over my shoulder.

'Ready!' I shouted. The broomstick propelled forward, and my feet lifted from the ground. As the clock chimed six, we flew straight through the open kitchen window and into a glorious sunset. My hair streamed out behind me and the coat billowed as we flew upwards and upwards, higher and higher into a darkening night sky where a ghostly moon hung suspended like a huge silver orb. When I felt brave enough to open both eyes to look down, OMG it looked so amazing. I could see our house far below, Lego-brick-sized. Seeing it gave me a strong pang of guilt. I thought about my mum.

'Bye, Mum. I hope I get back before you even know I've gone,' I whispered into the dark starlit sky. Wolfie howled in excitement and cried:

Slip the bonds of Earth and fly,
dipping gliding soaring high!

Chapter 14

It's hard to describe how thrilling it is to ride a broomstick!
Once you realise it's impossible to fall off and you dare to
look down, you lose your fear. Believe me, it's the most
exhilarating buzz ever. The views are breath-taking! The
moon illuminated the sky in a milky glow. We climbed
and circled, the wind whooshing by, my hair streaming out
behind me like a red banner.

'I'm flying!' I yelled, sticking my legs straight out.
'WOOHOOOO!' I shouted at the top of my voice. 'This is
epic! It's the best most stupendous adventure ever!'

Wolfie pricked up his ears and, sniffing the air,
he barked back at me. 'There's a storm coming. Hunker
down!'

I became aware of an eerie stillness. Ominous black
clouds drifted across the sky enshrouding the moon. As we
flew through their misty vapour I heard the first low rumble
of thunder. A streak of hot silver lightning split the sky.

'Hold on tight, Lia!' Wolfie shouted through the din
and crash of thunder. 'We have to make our way through
the eye of the storm.'

I knew enough to know that, if we were hit by
lightning, we would die!' I tried to remember the advice we
had been given at school.

To avoid being hit by lightning:

a. Do not stand in water – check.

b. Do not go near trees – check.

c. Be aware lightning always strikes at the highest point …

GULP!

A bolt of lightning tore across the sky. A great clap of thunder came too close. Torrential rain drove into us like needles. I ducked down, wishing it would stop.

As if my wish had been granted, and as suddenly as it started, it was over. The rain stopped, the clouds cleared, and the broomstick cruised onwards through a calm clear starlit sky.

The ordeal of the storm was over, but it had exhausted me. I felt myself dropping off. No! Duuuh! I don't mean I dropped off the broomstick. I mean I dropped off to sleep. Wolfie roused me to a sky streaked by the first rosy pink and gold hues of dawn.

'Lia, wake up we're going to be landing soon.' I rubbed sleep from my eyes while glancing down at the vast expanse of ocean below us.

'Wolfie, please tell me we're not landing in the sea!' I clutched his back. 'I have a fear of water. I can't swim!'

But before I could say anything more, a black swarm of ravens appeared as if from nowhere. They surrounded and flanked us and moving as one, twisting and turning, they guided and determined our direction.

'No need to be alarmed, Lia.' Wolfie reassured me. 'Ravens are known to bring about good passage. They've come to navigate and protect us.'

Soon the ravens left us and the broomstick began its

descent through the heavily clouded sky. I couldn't make out much below. A damp clammy mist obscured my view.

'Brace yourself!' Wolfie shouted.

I sucked in my breath and clenched my teeth, petrified.

As we hurtled downwards, I felt completely vulnerable. A mere speck against the dazzling vast blue ocean. I was certain we would plunge into the sea and drown, but without warning the broomstick turned sharply. It swerved to the right before nosediving steeply. As we hurtled down, I gripped the broomstick with one hand and covered my eyes with the other.

'Look below,' Wolfie coaxed.

I gave a quick glance down and spied far below us a green island enshrouded in shimmering sea mist. It appeared to float on the surface of the ocean.

Wolfie let out a long breath: 'Eynenholm Island.'

I peeped out from between my fingers, feeling relief when the broomstick slowed its descent. Seeing the ground below reassured me. The fields reminded me of small squares on a big map, then trees became visible. All was going well until we got caught up in strong crosswinds which blew us off course. We landed with a jolt, skiffing the surface of tough meadow grass until we were roughly thrown off and found ourselves in a heap right in the middle of a flock of grazing sheep. You can imagine their shock to find a wolf in their midst!

'Let's get out of here!' Wolfie barked as the sheep bleated in panic scattering in all directions.

Our feet sank into waterlogged boggy furrows

which slowed down our escape from the field. We scrambled through stinging nettles and tall prickled thistles until we came to a wooden stile. Keen to be out of the field of hysterical sheep, we vaulted over it and took a rutted path down towards the beach. A scent of wild garlic mingled with tangy sea smells drifted in the air. Early clumps of daffodils and banks of dainty snowdrops scattered along the hedgerows reminded me it was spring.

'Where's the broomstick? Did we leave it?' I looked back, scouring the field behind us.

'I sent it away,' Wolfie grunted.

When he saw my eyebrows shoot up, he defended his decision. 'It has a homing instinct. We're going to meet others at Sileby Castle. I know full well that, if I permitted it to come, it would only have caused mischief with the other broomsticks. I'm afraid I can't trust it to behave with any decorum. Don't worry, Lia, the broomstick will keep track of us. It will sense if it's needed. You can rely on that. Now we have to hurry. If the tide comes in any further, the causeway to the castle will become submerged and impassable.'

A thrill of anticipation tinged with apprehension ran through me. Soon I would be meeting with witches! I hoped Aurora had arrived safely and would be there to welcome us.

A silver crescent moon hung in the mid-afternoon sky casting a pale light over us as we hurried down to a deserted shingle beach. Raucous gannets disturbed the

peace, screeching and squawking as they swooped down to stab at mussel shells and dash them against the rocks.

The castle could only be reached via a narrow sandbar but already swishing waves were washing over it. Soon the access would be submerged and the castle cut off.

'Quick, there's no time to lose – the tide is coming in fast!' Wolfie spurred me on.

I picked up my skirts and began paddling through the soft wet sand, seawater lapping round my ankles. By the time we reached the small islet, I was wading knee-high in swirling water. We picked our way up the beach, careful not to slip on the green algae-covered rocks. The castle's landscaped gardens sloped down to meet the shoreline. We tramped up the steeply ridged path, and as we clambered to the top of the embankment a soft cooing of doves drifted down to us. I took in a deep breath, inhaling the pleasant aroma of spearmint. It wafted towards us from a herb garden where a girl, wearing a veiled helmet, was tending beehives.

Intent on her work, she didn't notice us. Wolfie gave a soft 'wuff' to attract her attention. She startled slightly and looked over in our direction. Removing her netted hat, she blinked in surprise, then, letting out a cry of recognition, she lay down the honeycomb she was holding and hurried towards us.

'Wolfie!' She raised her hand in greeting. Her expression was welcoming but had a hint of concern. I studied her from the corner of my eye. She looked to be around my age, pretty, with rosy cheeks and dark curls. She wasn't at all what I expected. I felt relieved to see she wore normal clothes, a white T-shirt, skinny jeans and sneakers, not the long black dress and cape I had imagined a witch would wear!

'We've been waiting on your mistress's arrival to begin the party,' the girl said. 'Where is she, Wolfie?' Her forehead creased. 'Oh sorry.' She blushed, her hand flying to her face. 'Where are my manners? We haven't been introduced. I'm Elspeth,' she gave me a wide grin, 'and you are Lia of course,' she nodded. 'We've been expecting you. You must be very...'

I interrupted her, 'Elspeth did you say Aurora isn't here? I stared at her. We thought she had gone on before us and would have arrived by now?'

'No she isn't here.' The girl frowned picking up on my anxiety. 'Come with me, we best go up and talk to the others.'

We fell in behind her following her up to the imposing castle rising up before us. Its battlements where banners must once have flown now grew long trailing grass and weeds. Its thick grey outer walls had long since fallen into dereliction and decay.

'This way.' She showed the way through a wide stone archway which led to a courtyard overshadowed by a large round tower.

'This is the keep,' she explained. 'It's the only part of the castle still intact.' She beckoned us to follow her up a worn stone stairway which led up to the keep's entrance.

'Wait, please,' I said, glancing down at myself, suddenly painfully aware of how I must look. 'I'm embarrassed to meet people wearing this.' I brushed my hand over the mud-splattered and torn red gown. 'I'd be much happier if I could wear my own clothes and just be myself.'

The corners of her mouth curled into a whimsical smile. 'I understand. Of course, you can. It's an easy matter.' She puckered her brow in concentration and

117

squeezed her eyes closed, murmuring something under her breath. In the blink of an eye, I stood in my own new hoodie, designer jeans, T-shirt and trainers.

Respect! I thought. She's one cool witch.

'We don't have any running water inside the castle, I'm afraid,' she apologised. 'We draw fresh water from the well in the courtyard.' She pointed it out to me. 'If you like, you could freshen up before coming up to join us?'

Her nose crinkled.

I checked my grimy hands grinning. 'Yeah, that would be a good idea!'

Wolfie and Elspeth climbed the remaining steps up to the castle entrance, leaving me in the courtyard. The well handle was heavy but I grasped and turned it, straining against its weight and managing to crank a bucket of water up to the surface. I put the brimming bucket on the rim of the well and leaned over to peer down into its inky-blue depths. As I trailed my fingers around the well edge, I noticed there were words of a rhyme engraved into the stone:

If you sacrifice something you hold dear,
Your wish will be granted,
the future made clear.
The messengers dressed in
black and white
Come not by foot but via flight.
One's a bad omen, but good luck is two;
In their number your future's
imparted to you.

Pondering on this riddle, I attempted to solve its meaning. If I gave up something important to me, I would be able to see into the future? Would that help me find Aurora? I touched the precious necklace around my neck. It was something dear to me. I had promised Aurora I would a wear it always. Should I sacrifice it for a glimpse of the future? Would it show me where to find her? I attempted tapping into my sixth sense hoping to find answers but I knew it didn't work like that. It wouldn't be summoned at will. Making a quick decision I unclasped the necklace and held it a moment, dangling it over the well, admiring the way it glistened in the light. From the corner of my eye, I caught a glimpse of something black and white flutter overhead. A magpie! It spotted my necklace sparkle and flew down and snatched it from my hand.

'Hey!' I yelled as it flew off, gripping my necklace in its beak. The thieving bird landed on a ledge beside its partner, pausing a moment before flying down again and perching beside me. Cocking its head, it dropped something into the bucket, fixed me with its beady eye, then finally flew off.

A little blue opaque glass bottle stopped with a cork floated on the water's surface. I fished it out and prised out the rolled-up paper wedged inside. It read:

Your messengers dressed in
black and white
Come not by foot, but come by flight,
One's a bad omen, good luck is two,
The vision makes clear what you must do.

The rhyme's meaning became clear. Two magpies had visited me, and they had brought me a message!

Chapter 15

Something else glimmered blue in the bucket. I dipped my fingers into the water to fetch it out. My necklace! As I moved my fingers around the surface, the water began to ripple. Intriguingly, a blurry image began to take shape. My eyes strained, peering into the water's inky depths. It swirled around in the bucket, taking on the same colour as the water in the well. A shade of deep sapphire blue.

The reflection showed me a shadowy gloomy place resembling the inside of a dark cave. Slowly, bit by bit the image became less cloudy and finally a crystal-clear vision of Aurora emerged. She sat alone in a dark shadowy place imprisoned by bars of glittering black ice.

I leaned over the bucket and called out her name: 'Aurora.' She lifted her chin and tilted her head as if listening, then the vision faded.

Dipping my fingers into the water, I fished out my necklace and clasped it around my neck. Hardly able to contain myself, I ran to the castle taking the high stone steps two at a time in my rush to get to Wolfie. It took a huge effort to push open the heavy entrance door of the great circular hall, and as I warily stepped inside a strong aroma of herbs mingled with wood smoke caught the back of my throat and made my eyes sting. Dripping wax candles glimmered from wall sconces, bathing the hall in a soft, muted light. As my eyes adjusted to their subdued flicker I could make out several women at the far end of the hall seated on benches arranged around an ornate open fireplace. I felt self-conscious and clumsy walking the length of this great hall, sure all eyes were scrutinising me. I could see there had been considerable preparations for the Ostara celebrations. I passed down the middle of two long trestle tables covered in white cloths and I breathed in the sweet scent from vases brim full of spring flowers – narcissi, hyacinths and cherry blossom. Colourful banners had been hung from the rafters heralding the coming of spring.

Wolfie spotted me and rose immediately from his warm spot on the hearth in front of the blazing fire. He bowed his head to me and came to stand by my side.

'We have to assume the worst has happened Lia.' He dropped his head.

'I have something I need to share with you, Wolfie. I've been shown a …'

Just as I was about to share my vision with him the beekeeping girl, Elspeth, hurried over.

'Lia.' She took my hand. 'My but you are cold! Please come over and sit with us by the fire.'

She took my arm and led me over to a group of women, some young, some old. All looked perfectly normal, not at all spooky. They immediately gathered around fussing over me. A cheery, round-faced little woman gripped my hand in hers.

'Ah, Lia. Aurora has told us so much about you. We've been looking forward to meeting you.' I felt too shy to make conversation, so I laid my satchel down and stood warming myself by the fire feeling awkward. I was bursting to tell Wolfie about the things the vision had shown me.

Wolfie settled down again and sprawling out on the fireside rug he gave a long contented sigh.

'Wolfie!' I nudged him with my foot. 'Don't go to sleep! We need to talk about ...'

Before I could finish the plump woman clapped her hands for silence.

She beamed me a wide smile. 'We're delighted you're here, Lia. Come. Sit here by me ... Meg, get down!'

She pushed a black cat off the bench. As its paws touched the flagstones I stared in disbelief as it transformed into a dark-haired girl!

'Purr!' she said, giving me a wide Cheshire-cat grin. 'I'm Megan.' Then seeing my bafflement, she laughed. 'Oh, don't mind me I'm always up to mischief. Please.' She patted the seat. 'Do sit down. You look worn out.'

The plump woman's eyes twinkled. 'Megan, you're a rascal.' She stoked the fire and tinkled a little bell. 'Please gather round, ladies. I'm afraid there's some extremely worrying news.'

After an exchange of concerned murmuring, the women took their seats around the fireside and gave me their full attention.

'I'm sorry to be bringing you bad news ...' I fiddled with my cuff. '... I guess I'll just have to come out with it.' In a barely audible voice I whispered, 'You all know Aurora hasn't arrived here so we have to assume she's gone missing.'

Everyone spoke at once.

'Shhh!' Elspeth said, raising her hand. 'Quiet, please. We should listen to what Lia has to say.'

One of my pet hates is being the centre of attention, but this situation required me to step up. I drew in a long breath and began to speak in a stronger voice.

'I was to come with Aurora here to Eynenholm Island to join you for the celebrations. She was very specific I should arrive early so that we could set off in good time. When Wolfie and I arrived at her home, her house looked as though it had been ransacked. She was nowhere to be found.' My voice faltered. 'We wondered if she had set off accidentally early when trying out a new teleportation spell, but if that's the case she hasn't arrived safely. I'm afraid something very bad has happened to her.' I held back my tears.

'So she's disappeared without trace?' The women's eyes widened.

My eyes darted around their shocked faces. Could I trust them? Should I tell them of the strange vision I'd had at the well? I had no choice. I spoke out.

'Today in the courtyard I was given a message. A revelation.'

Wolfie's eyes focused intently on me.

'Aurora is being held against her will somewhere dark … and frightening.'

Sybil, the plump woman sitting beside me, jumped to her feet. Her eyes showed fear as she uttered one word. 'TYRA!'

A collective outcry prompted her to bang the flat of the table with her hand.

'Please, everyone be quiet. But was it Aurora who

made contact with you, Lia?' Her eyes narrowed. 'Or was that Tyra's doing?'

Her eyes cast around the room. 'Could it be a trick to lure the girl?' Her lips pressed together in a grim line.

'I don't know for sure.' I lowered my eyes to hide my apprehension. 'But I do know I have to find Aurora and go to her. She needs my help.'

Sybil shook her head focusing worried eyes on me and said.

'My dear you must not do anything rash.' Her eyes flickered past me to the listening women, seeking their approval to continue. 'Tyra is a villainous creature. She rules over an evil kingdom of spirits who cannot be appeased or reasoned with. Wickedness and harm are their sole objectives. You will not be safe in her realm.' She placed both hands flat on the table and leaned in towards me, her face grave. 'Tyra means to destroy you.'

Wolfie rose and came to stand by my side. His amber eyes flared like torches. Assessing the mood in the room he spoke in a resonant tone.

'As you all know, it is in my nature to be loyal. When it comes to matters of protecting my mistress I am the most relentless creature you will ever know. I am not naive. I know there will be great risks, but I choose not to think about all the reasons I could fail her. I chose to focus on the reasons I will not fail her. We will leave immediately.'

Sybil studied him a moment then, accepting his decision, bowed her head.

'Very well, if you are not going to be persuaded out of it, perhaps we can help to keep you safe.'

One by one the women rose and came to me. Introducing themselves they gave me their gifts.

Elspeth, placing a green jade stone in my lap, said shyly, 'To protect you on a journey.'

Ariana, a slight, shy girl, pressed a small blue stone into my hand: 'This is agate, a stone for good fortune and courage.'

Matilda gave me a blend of oils. When I uncorked the bottle, the smell of cedarwood made tears well up in my eyes. It took me back to the warmth of Aurora's kitchen and to the feelings of love I had for her.

Winifred gave me a red garnet stone. Blinking owlishly, she explained: 'To calm anxiety, dear.'

Thea knelt down and offered me a malachite gemstone which she cupped in her hands: 'To help overcome obstacles and challenges.'

Ariana speaking in a lilting voice gave me a little sachet of herbs: 'Bay leaf for protection and dandelion for interaction with the spirits.'

Ellyn gave me a candle: 'To light your way.' Her strange pale eyes studied me.

Jocelyn placed a light hand on my shoulder. She gave me three raven's feathers 'to represent air and safe flight'.

Sybil held out a crystal: 'to transmit energy,' she explained, touching its sharp tip. 'You can use this point to direct positive energy to the spirit realm.'

Dame Edith pressed a tiger's eye stone into my hand: 'For strength and confidence.' She patted my hand.

Rose placed a little glass jar in my lap. When I picked it up, I saw that its contents glowed white. 'It's a healing spell,' she explained, looking at me with round eyes, 'though, of course, my hope is you will not need to use it.'

Finally, Megan came to me and squeezed a silver

cat charm into my palm. 'You might need this to ward off evil. Its magic is very potent. It will help bring you back safe.' Her green feline eyes studied mine.

I took their gifts with grateful thanks and placed them into the satchel. Without further delay, we all trooped down the stone steps and out into the courtyard. I stood on the shoreline taking deep breaths of salty sea air as I tried to calm myself. I have to admit I felt very afraid of what might come. Did I have the strength to do this? As always, Wolfie, always intuitive to my thoughts, sensed my misgivings.

'It's all right to be scared,' he whispered. 'Being scared means you're about to do something really brave.' A movement in the bed of seaweed at my feet caught my eye. The broomstick had returned.

'So there is no misunderstanding, my bristly friend,' Wolfie warned, standing over it. 'You will take us directly to Elfhame Island. If you fail us, I promise that you will be banished to a barn to sweep cobwebs forevermore.'

I swung the satchel over my shoulder and said my final thanks. Wolfie and I wished the assembled witches goodbye.

Megan stepped forward and clasped my arm. 'Take good care of yourself, Lia. We'll delay the celebrations until you bring Aurora back to us.'

The broomstick swished back and forth, impatient to go. This time I had no fear of flying. As dawn broke, we took off, flying through sun-lit clouds which drifted across a gold-tinted morning sky.

Chapter 16

We flew over swathes of blue-green pine forests bordering a patchwork of green-and-yellow countryside. When the sun rose fully it flooded the sky in a burst of golden brilliance. Somehow the broomstick managed to get us caught up in the midst of an arrow of honking geese cruising the skies searching for new feeding grounds. This mishap confused its radar and made it abruptly lose height. Unexpectedly, it also began to shake and shudder so violently I was almost thrown off.

'What's happening? I panicked, shouting into the wind.

'The broomstick has lost its sense of direction.' Wolfie growled in exasperation.'

Just as the broomstick steadied the wind picked up and buffeted and battered us with such force it blew us completely off course.

'Brace yourself!' Wolfie shouted. 'We'll have to make an emergency landing!'

I screwed my eyes tight shut and clenched my jaw.

'Ahhrrrg!' I sucked in my breath as the broomstick plummeted earthwards. I gripped the broomstick with white knuckles and, dropping my head, gritted my teeth. For a moment it seemed we were doomed, but thankfully the broomstick braked violently just before we hit the ground. It bounced and skimmed the bumpy surface, abruptly jettisoning us off into hummocks of long seagrass. Trembling all over, I stood up on shaky legs and checked to see if I was still in one piece.

'Wolfie, are you all right?' I said through chattering teeth. He rose onto all four paws, circled a couple of times, and shook himself.

'That was close,' he panted. 'Where has the cursed thing landed us?'

I strained to see through thick briny mist and took a few steps forward.

'Stop right there!' Wolfie barked at me. I looked down and froze, teetering on the very edge of a clifftop, a sheer drop below me. The raging ocean crashed against the rocks far below.

'The broomstick's dumped us here in the middle of nowhere.' His lip curled. 'The wee feardie's skedaddled!'

'You mean it's just gone?'

'A good thing, too,' he snarled. 'If I got my teeth into that scunner of a broomstick, I'd chew it into a thousand matchsticks. Come on,' he wuffed. 'We won't get anywhere just sitting here.' He began sniffing his way down a steep winding path. 'We better see where this leads.'

We followed the overgrown path until it eventually petered out in front of a faded blue, five-barred gate. It was precariously fixed into the ground by wooden posts just a few steps from the edge of the cliff. Beyond it was a step into nothingness and a long drop into the ocean. The sign hanging from the gate, distorted and dulled by age, read:

Its hinges and nails were rusted over by salty air, giving me the impression one good gust of wind could blow it over but when I tried to push it open it wouldn't budge.

I flopped down on the wet grass and gave a half shrug, 'It doesn't make sense. Why would someone build a gate here? What a waste of time! It's a dead-end leading to nowhere. Come on.' I jumped up, impatient to go. 'There's nothing here.'

Wolfie stared up at the sky his eyes tracking something. 'Look!' he urged.

An eagle flying against the headwinds soared overhead. Spreading its great wings and beating the air, it dived and swooped above us.

'Awesome.' I said, gazing up at it.

'It's a sign.' Wolfie focused on the magnificent bird circling above us.

'The eagle symbolises courage, strength and the freedom to look ahead. He's been summoned for a reason. I'm sure of it.'

The eagle circled once more then flew down towards us. Alighting on the gate, he fixed small bright eyes on me. Fluffing out his wings he moved from foot to foot, dropping a leather pouch on the grass.

'I knew it! Wolfie nodded. 'He's brought us a message. Go on, Lia. Open it.'

Inside the pouch, I found a scroll written in fine script:

To pass through this gate,
one word is the key –
The password's not hidden,
it's obvious, you see.
You doubt yourself now
but know it is true,
There's powerful magic inside of you.
Your special gifts come to the fore –
A wolf will teach you magic lore.

The eagle cocked his head from side to side, watching me intently.

'It's a riddle.' Wolfie explained. 'We have to guess the password which will allow us through this gate. The eagle is showing us the way.'

'Pass through the gate?' I said in disbelief. 'Are you crazy! There's nothing at the other side of this gate but a sheer drop!' I took a tentative step to the cliff edge and stared down at the waves crashing on the rocks far below. The drop made my stomach lurch. I shrank back from the edge and turned away, folding my arms. 'No way! I'm not doing it!'

Wolfie began to pace. 'It isn't about passing through this gate, though, is it? It's an important test of your courage. Are you strong enough to face the challenges ahead? If you can't do this, then now is the time to turn back, though' – his eyes rested on mine – 'it would be a great pity. Remember Aurora's teachings. If you believe in yourself enough, you can do anything. You have the makings of a great and powerful witch.'

'All right! You don't need to say any more.' I levelled a glowering look at him. 'I'm not giving up! I'll do it! We need to guess the password, right? I'm good at solving puzzles and riddles.'

I made a couple of guesses. 'Journey? Open Sesame? Abracadabra?' After several more attempts, the gate hadn't budged. I chewed on my lower lip and said, 'I must be missing something obvious.' The eagle became excited and, loosening his grasp on his perch, he fluttered down to my feet. Fixing me with his beady eye, he gave a high-pitched cry. He's trying to tell me something. I read through the riddle again. Then it dawned on me! The password's not hidden, it's obvious, you see. Yes! That's it!

'It's obvious! Wolfie!' I yelled, punching the air. I placed a hand on the gate and said, 'The password is OBVIOUS!'

Inch by inch it scraped open. I passed through it and stood tottering on the edge of the cliff, hardly daring to look down at the sheer drop. 'I don't think I can climb down the cliff face, Wolfie.' I panicked. 'It looks much too steep and dangerous.'

'I agree.' Wolfie nodded. 'You can't climb down.'

'Phew, that's a relief. Can we go back now?'

Wolfie gave me a long look. 'Sometimes you have to take a leap of faith, Lia. Your wings already exist. All you have to do is fly.'

'You're telling me I can fly?'

'You have to trust in yourself.'

'You think my magic is powerful enough for me to fly?' I asked again.

133

'I know the only way we can go forward is if you believe in yourself enough to take this step, but you have to make your choice.' His eyes glinted. 'Mortal or magic? You decide.'

I gazed down at the huge drop below, feeling dizzy. I knew taking this step was a test. If I trusted myself enough to step into the void, it would be my final step towards acceptance of my supernatural powers. It would pledge me to live my life as a witch. The eagle took wing and hovered, hanging in the air waiting for me. A compelling inner voice urged me on–'Take this step into your destiny.' I knew now with certainty what I must do and felt sure I could channel the spirit of this mighty bird. My decision was made. I turned frightened eyes to Wolfie. His jaw tightened.

'You can do this, Lia!'

Gritting my teeth and squeezing my eyes closed, I took a step into the abyss. Astonishingly, instead of plummeting down I felt myself floating. The eagle encircled me and took me with him into an updraft where we rode warm air currents flying from thermal to thermal. I spiralled downwards like a feather being carried on a warm breeze, until I landed safely and gently on the sandy shore.

'Woah! That was epic!' I breathed, feeling elation. The eagle left me then, soaring high until he was no more than a speck in the blue sky. I understood in that moment I had taken an irreversible step towards my destiny. There was no going back now.

As I gazed up at the towering cliff rising sharply behind me, I spotted Wolfie surefootedly loping down its narrow stringy paths.

'I did it, Wolfie!' I shouted to him as he bounded along the shore towards me. 'I flew! It was sooo amazing! I want to do it again!' I laughed, hugging myself. He flopped down on the sand beside me, praising me. 'Well done, Lia, for believing in yourself.'

As we sat together in companionable silence just listening to the placid waves dousing the shoreline in white froth, a slight chill in the air made me shiver. Something in the stillness, in the eerie quality of the light, in the sea's unnatural calm gave me a creepy feeling. My sixth sense came to the fore, warning me of something ominous.

'Do you feel spooked too, Wolfie?' I turned to him, catching his uneasy expression.

'What is it, Wolfie?' I said, trying to keep the tremor from my voice. I ran my hand down his back, feeling him quiver as he kept his eyes firmly on the horizon.

'There lies Elfhame Island. Tyra's domain,' he growled.

I followed his gaze to the distant outline of a large island sitting in the middle of the ocean surrounded by deep blue-indigo waters. It appeared to drift mysteriously just above the surface. We sat contemplating it until it became hidden, shrouded in vaporous dark purple mist.

Chapter 17

'We have to be stealthy. We daren't draw attention to our presence. Elfhame Island is a dangerous unholy place,' Wolfie stressed, pacing back and forth.

'It is a colony of dishonourable faerie folk who have fallen from grace. They are thoroughly wicked. You have to be aware, Lia, they are demoniac creatures who take on many guises. They are without conscience or ethics. They have even been known to steal children whom they think will not be missed, carrying them off in a whirlwind of dust.'

'You're frightening me!' I said, swallowing hard and blinking.

His forehead creased in a frown. 'I have to make you understand the wickedness your adversary is capable of. Some say Tyra is the devil in the shape of a woman. She rules her realm from subterranean caves. Concealed from the upper world she vents her fury against mortals by raising deadly storms, making widows of fishermen's wives.

We scrunched over the gritty sand, making our way down the beach to the ocean's edge. Powerful gusts of wind blew up a sandstorm. I muffled myself inside Aurora's coat, shielding myself from the grainy particles that were blowing into my face. The afternoon light had faded to an eerie gloom, turning the sky to shades of deep indigo and purple. As the light faded, so, too, did any warmth, leaving only a raw chilliness.

As we stood on the shore scanning the horizon, Wolfie's ears pricked. He stood stock-still, intent on listening.

A rhythmic noise rose above the sound of the sea, louder than the crash of waves pounding the shore, louder than the howling wind. The hairs on the back of my neck prickled. Something fearsome was out there! Wolfie tensed, and sniffing the air he stiffened, his hackles up. We stood transfixed, watching as a luminous glow formed where the sea shifted and parted, and from it the ghostly spectre of a magnificent white stallion broke through the white-crested waves and galloped furiously towards us.

Wolfie's eyes widened, his ears flattened. With a deep vibrating growl, he turned tail. 'Follow me, Lia. Move back into the shadows ... now!'

We ran and hid in the shelter of the dunes, where I huddled into Wolfie, burying my face in his thick pelt. I only dared to glimpse the horse galloping crazily through the tossing waves, its thundering hooves flying, arching spray. With its nostrils flaring, the horse reared up and turned abruptly to the shore barrelling towards us, and all at once it was only metres away. I could clearly see the smooth lines of its powerful body as fluid as the water it came from. I could almost feel its hot breath like plumes of white smoke escaping its nostrils.

Then it was on us! Wolfie drew his lips back in a snarl as the horse reared over him, lashing out dangerously with deadly pawing hooves. I had to stop it. Think! I fumbled for the silver charm of protection Megan had given me and clutching it in my trembling hand, I forced

myself to my feet. I stood trembling on shaking legs
and dug deep inside myself. I balled my hands into fists
and spoke to the inner part of me where my magic lives.
Focusing intensely on my will and my desire, my voice
rang out clear and commanding:

Rise to the surface. Empower me!

I squeezed my eyes shut riveting my concentration
on my intention:

*I cast a spell of intervention to call upon
the forces of good. I entreat you,
do my bidding. Create a protective shield
around me. Let nothing harm me!*

Rooting myself to the spot, I stood my ground
in front of the pawing, rearing stallion. I inhaled a sharp
breath and hurled a further command. Holding the flat of
my palm up to the rearing beast, and in the most forceful
voice I could muster I roared:

DESIST!

The mighty horse's ears flattened, it rolled its eyes,
its nostrils flared, and with a rumbling snort, it whirled
and turned back to the ocean. Galloping like wildfire,
its mane and tail streaming, it plunged back into the sea,
disappearing in a fountain of spume. Foaming white waves
like rearing wild horses engulfed him.

'I was afraid I would fail.'

My legs turned limp and I collapsed where I stood,
crumpling in a heap on the churned-up sand. Wolfie circled

and dropped down beside me.

'Ah, but you didn't fail, Lia. Tyra sent her emissary as a warning,' he growled, 'but you've sent her back a powerful message. Your magic is as strong as hers.' His gaze swung out to sea, focusing on the dark sinister island overcast in glowering shadow.

'She knows we're here. We must stay below her detection. She mustn't know our movements. It could put Aurora at terrible risk.'

'I understand.' I clasped my arms around my knees, rocking back and forth. But how can we get to the island without being detected? 'Should we call the broomstick back?' I suggested.

Wolfie gave a mirthless laugh and shook his head.

'We can't trust that accursed scallywag. No. We have to think of another way.'

I stroked my chin. 'Could we use magic to instantly transport us to the island?'

He shook his big head. 'Risky. No, that won't work,' he explained. 'Too uncertain. We couldn't be sure where we would pitch up. We must keep below Tyra's sights.' His eyes wandered out to the ocean. 'We will cross over to the island by sea.'

I shot him a sceptical look. 'But how?'

He rolled his eyes in exasperation. 'By boat, of course!'

'But we can't. We don't have a boat.' I shrugged.

'Have you learned nothing, Lia? There's no such word as "can't" in the world of magic.' Disapproval flashed in his eyes. 'Conjure one!'

'Huh!' I scowled. 'It's not that straightforward.'

Huffily I turned away from him and taking the spell book from the satchel, I began leafing through it.

'It's no good. I don't understand it.' I grumbled. 'It's mumbo-jumbo to me.' I threw Wolfie a look of frustration and tossed the spell book at him. 'How am I supposed to understand those weird symbols?'

'Let me look,' he sighed, nosing into the pages.

'No. I can do it.' I glared at him. 'I'm going to work this out myself!' I yanked the book back and studied the book again. 'There's a spell for crossing water, and there's a spell for navigating the ocean safely. Which one should I try?'

'Both?' He lifted his shoulders in a shrug.'

$$ \maltese \quad \text{\textsection} \quad \boxed{\text{不}} \quad \aleph \quad \maltese $$

I crossed my fingers for luck and repeated the spell for crossing water, changing it slightly substituting by the word 'water' for 'sea.' I waited expectantly, searching the shallows in the hope a sailing boat would materialise, but instead, in response to my spell, a pod of dolphins emerged from the blue depths. Playfully riding the waves, leaping high, two of them split away from the pod, and squealing and arcing their tails they turned their shiny heads towards us. They moved smoothly through the deep water and glided into the shallows.

'You've evoked a spell to cross the sea but not in a boat!' Wolfie howled. 'Come on!' He jerked his head in the direction of the sea. Half buried in spray he plunged into the rippling ocean and jumped astride a dolphin's back.

'Woooah. No!' I threw my hands in the air. 'I can't swim!'

He blew out his cheeks. 'Now you tell me! But you won't have to swim! The dolphins will carry us safely across to the island.'

I drew in a deep breath of tangy sea air and waded out until the ocean's swell lifted my feet from the sandy seabed. One of the dolphins swam up alongside me and I easily hoisted myself onto his smooth grey rubbery back. When I was safely astride, the dolphin began to chatter fishy language to me, allowing me to grasp its fin. I held on tight while we were being propelled forward by the current. (By the way, all the things you've ever heard about swimming with dolphins are true. It's incredible!)

I gave Wolfie the thumbs-up!

'Wooo-hooo!' I hollered. 'This is phenomenal!'

Twisting and turning our way through the water, we glided smoothly through green unfathomable depths towards the darkly ominous Elfhame Island.

Chapter 18

As the distance narrowed between ourselves and the island, the dolphins, sensing danger, expressed their fear to each other using a series of high whistling and clicking noises. They were clearly unwilling to take us any further: using their tails they slapped the surface of the water to communicate their intention to each other, then, in unison, unceremoniously pitched us off into the sea. I watched in dismay as their sleek bodies pushed fast through the water, their dorsal fins slipping in and out of the waves as they headed away from us, back out into deep water.

The sea was sucking me under. I floundered, fighting to stay afloat, kicking and flailing, gulping in mouthfuls of salty water, unable to prevent myself from sinking down, down, down into a watery silence. When it felt as though I couldn't hold my breath a second longer my feet touched sediment on the seabed. I snapped my eyes open and peered into the inky blue-green dimly lit ocean floor. Letting go of my breath I felt huge astonishment to find I was able to breathe underwater! I began to swim through this watery kingdom and soon became surrounded by a shoal of little silverfish. They swam with me along the seabed in and out of coral-encrusted rock tunnels and stayed with me guiding me up and upwards until I could see a point of light above. I broke through the surface with a huge gasp and gave in to the sensation of just floating through beds of gently swaying seaweed, the long fronds drifting and curling around my body. The tides took me to the shallows and washed me up on to the beach like a piece of flotsam.

Feeling exhausted by my ordeal, I sprawled out on the sand to rest a while, and, as soon as I recovered, I propped myself up on my elbows scanning the wide expanse of shore-line. The sight of a large grey creature bounding up the beach towards me caused me to get ready to run. I stumbled backwards as with a great thrusting leap it hurled its great wet hairy body at me.

'Woooah! Wolfie. It's you! Stop it. You're covering me in sand!'

'Are you all right?' he panted into my face, his ears laid back uncertainly. 'I was afraid you had drowned.'

'You gave me an awful fright,' I said in a shaky voice. I thought you were a sea-monster.'

'Sorry, I didn't mean to scare you,' he panted.

'I know. It's all right.' I gave a dismissive wave of my hand. 'I'm just glad you're safe. Wolfie do you want to know something incredible? I can breathe underwater! It's so cool!'

He shook himself, drenching me in water droplets, then circled several times before he dropped to the ground beside me. Curling himself into a wet lump he rested his head on his paws and yawned. 'It's not so surprising, Lia. Or did you forget you're descended from mermaids?'

He stretched out on the sand beside me, and I realised he had fallen asleep when he gave a great snorting snore. His nose was mashed against the sand in a most uncomfortable-looking manner, but I guess I knew him well enough by now to know that he could sleep anywhere.

'Wolfie,' I nudged him awake. Opening one eye he blinked and stretched out his front paws.

'Sorry, I must have dropped off,' he wuffed. Now fully awake he became conscious of our predicament, abruptly sitting up and scratching his ear vigorously with his hind paw. His ears pricked, his eyes wary, he was alert, vigilant for any movement.

'We can't stay here.' He stiffened, sniffing the air. 'It's not safe ... Too exposed.'

'Which way should we go?' I scanned our surroundings. Tall shaded pines stretching to the sky like dark-green arrows hemmed the perimeter of the bay. Beyond them far in the distance, a huge natural rock formation loomed large, overshadowing the landscape, its pitted caves like yawning, gaping mouths.

'We'll take cover in the forest.' His eyes flickered past me to the densely packed trees. 'It's safer.'

'I thought there was a reason you avoided going into forests?' I eyed him in surprise. 'Aurora told me that years ago you'd had a frightening experience.'

His eyes sloped down at the corners like a frightened pup. I could tell the memory of whatever had happened to him still scared him.

'What happened to you?' I probed in a gentle voice.

'One of those days I'll tell you but not now,' he replied and, keeping his nose to the ground, he slunk off in the direction of the forest, his tail tucked between his legs.

A green scent of pine met us as we stepped into the shaded shelter of the woodland. We crossed over its threshold into a thicket of densely packed trees, their canopy almost shutting out daylight. My skin prickled. It felt eerily quiet. No sound of birdsong here, only the sound of the wind sighing through the trees.

'This place frightens me,' I whispered, blinking my eyes several times as I tried to adjust to the gloom.

'Aye,' he agreed. 'Stay close to me. Without a doubt, malevolent forces dwell here. We are in dangerous territory. An unholy alliance of faerie folk who are disgraced and punished for wrongful use of their magic inhabit this forest.

'What have they done?' I felt my spine tingle.

'They are guilty of misguiding and disrupting the process of nature and bringing harm to humans and to the Earth.'

I shrank closer to him. 'Are they here watching us?' My eyes darted all around.

He grimaced and nodded. 'You may not see them but they are here. They dislike intrusion intensely.' His eyes narrowed. 'Take care, Lia, the ground is boggy here. There is a danger you could be sucked down by quicksand. Worse,' – he shifted his gaze to a wide circle of fungus growing in the mossy forest floor – 'you must never step within a fairy ring. Be aware. Some spirits will fool you with their antics and entice you to go with them into their ring, some will lure you with promises. Beware of their trickery. They will ensnare you with enchantment and enslave you for ever.'

In my fright, I stumbled and tripped over a knotted root and almost lost my footing.

'Have I not just cautioned you?' he growled. 'Take great care where you step!' He shot me a warning look.

'Woe betide anyone who disturbs a fairy path. If you were to accidentally destroy it, you would invite their terrible wrath. They would curse you!'

'I understand,' I said in a strained voice. I stayed close behind him, keeping my eyes down, vigilant.

As we moved deeper into the forest's gloom, the twisting path became more difficult to follow. I sensed Wolfie's presence rather than saw him. His colouring against the long dark shadows gave him perfect camouflage.

When night fell a pale moon cast weak thin slivers of light through the black silhouetted trees. 'Wolfie,' I whispered into the darkness, 'I can't see you. I'm afraid we'll get separated.'

When his coat brushed against my leg I put my hand down, clutching at his ruff, keeping a tight hold on him. I whimpered, 'I'm frightened. I can't see. Can we hole up somewhere until it gets light?' I felt him move away.

'Don't leave me!' I panicked.

'I'm here,' he reassured me. He nudged his nose under my hand and, with a light grip, he took my hand in his muzzle and guided me through the pitch dark to an ancient tree, its roots twisted and intertwined like gnarled fingers gripping the forest floor. I leaned against its thick trunk feeling protected, comforted by its mighty size. In that moment the moon slid out from behind dense cloud casting the forest in a pale milky glow.

'Look.' Wolfie's eyes gleamed. 'The tree has a large hollow. Climb in. I'll stand guard.'

I curled myself into the tree's cavity, cowering down in fright. Distorted shapes of twisted tree branches loomed out at me from creeping tendrils of mist. Somewhere close by a twig snapped.

'What was that?' My breath quickened. 'Wolfie, are you still there?'

'I'm right here,' he grunted.

I clambered out of the tree hollow and snuggled up beside him, feeling better for having him close to me.

'I'm too scared to sleep,' I said, trembling. His eyes glowed amber in the dark.' It's not the most comfortable place I've ever spent the night in, but we've no choice – we have to stay here until first light.'

'Wolfie, remember you promised to tell me your story?'

He gave a soft wuff. 'Which story is that? There are so many.'

'You promised you would tell me the story of how you became Aurora's wolf?' I coaxed.

He sat up, yawned and scratched his ear. 'Aye, it's an interesting story right enough.' The corners of his mouth twitched. 'And I guess it'll help pass this long night.'

Chapter 19

Wolfie curled up beside me. 'Did you know fairy tales and fables sometimes come from true events, Lia?'

'No, I didn't know that, Wolfie.'

'I don't wish to sound immodest,' he continued, 'but I am a legend.'

I burst out laughing. 'Being a legend means you're famous, doesn't it?'

'Exactly,' he replied, 'I am famous!'

'Tell me how you're famous.' I relaxed back onto a mound of leaves, eager to hear his tale.

'Let me see.' He tilted his head, 'Back in 1697 a man named Charles Perrault heard of my story and wrote it down. It's been passed down through the ages from generation to generation, although ...' Wolfie snorted '... he did distort some of the facts and he changed the ending, which I'm sorry to say gave the grey wolf a bad reputation.'

'Do you mean the "big bad wolf" thing?' I turned to him, propping my head up on my elbow.

'Aye,' he tutted. 'It is an unfair description. I will now put the record straight. I suppose you could say I'm a rescue wolf because Aurora rescued me a long time ago. As I've already explained, way back in the severe winter of 1645 a bloody battle drove my pack deep into the forest.

That is when I became separated from them. I had to learn to hunt and forage by myself. Conditions were harsh, food scarce.' His voice faltered. 'I grew weak. I almost starved to death.'

Recalling those painful memories obviously caused him distress. I stroked his head to comfort him.

'How did you survive?' I gently prompted him.

He cleared his throat. 'Hurrruph. One morning while out in the forest searching for food I spied a young girl wrapped in a crimson-coloured cloak struggling and slipping her way along an icy footpath. She was carrying a heavy basket which my nose informed me contained food. I hoped there might be a chance she'd spare me some, so I bounded over and gave her my most charming wolfish grin.

'"Good day to you, bonnie lass. Might I ask your name and where you're bound this bleak winter's day? Can I be of assistance? Are you lost?" I tried to sound reassuring but I could see she was afraid of me. "No cause for alarm, my dear. I'm a friendly beastie. I mean you no harm." I eyed her basket, licking my lips.

'She hopped from foot to foot anxious to be on her way. Tugging her red cloak tight around herself, she answered in a small timid voice. "My name's Scarlett. Thank you for asking, but no, I'm not lost." She shook her golden curls. My mother sent me to Grandmama's house with some provisions." She glanced down at her basket. "My Grandma lives not far from here by Tumblers Hollow." She pointed. "Over in that direction. My mother is worried about my grandmama." Scarlett blinked. 'She is old and her home is snowbound." She forced a small smile. "Please may I go now? She needs me to take her supplies."

'"Yes, I see! My eyes lit up." I knew it. She had

food! Trying not to appear overly eager I took a step towards her. "May I walk with you? I could guard you," I said with a wink. "I'm good company. I know lots of good jokes!"

'Her face flushed. 'No, thank you," she said, gripping her basket firmly. "I prefer to travel alone." With that, she turned on her heel and hurried away.'

'I remember how the fairy tale goes.' I wrinkled my nose. 'But it was just a made-up story; it wasn't true, was it, Wolfie?'

He winced. 'I'm afraid it's all true. You could say it was at this is the point everything went terribly wrong.' A muscle in his jaw twitched. 'I decided to lope on ahead to check on her granny.' He glanced sideways at me. 'Just to make sure she was all right, you understand.'

'Of course.' I nodded.

'I took a short cut and arrived at her grandmother's cottage to find people were already there. I slipped into the shadows and watched her being helped into a horse-drawn cart. I realised they were villagers there to rescue her. She was driven away, I guessed to safety.

'Och jings! No breakfast for me now, I thought, feeling desperate. Unless … Did you know wolves are great pranksters, Lia?' Wolfie's eyes twinkled. Giving me a sheepish grin, he continued his tale.

'I let myself into Granny's cottage, thinking it would be funny to put on her nightshirt and nightcap and wait for Scarlett. I planned to jump out of bed and give her a bit of a fright, just for a joke.'

My eyebrows shot up. 'Not a very good joke.'

He gave a bitter laugh. 'I thought she would see the funny side of it. I always intended to explain right away that her granny had been taken to the safety of the village.

153

I thought when she was reassured and we were on friendly terms I would ask Scarlett to share her food with a starving wolf.' He gave a half-shrug and shook his head. 'I don't know how I could have been so naive. I'm embarrassed to tell you the next part of the story.'

'I think I know what happened.' I shook my head. 'But go on,' I urged him, anticipating what was coming next.

He sighed. 'I climbed into Granny's bed, put on her specs and settled down to wait. Before long I heard the click of the latch and the door opening.'

"Granny. It's me – Scarlett."

'I pulled the bed covers up around my head and said in a muffled voice, "Come in, Scarlett dear. I'm keeping warm in bed."'

'You rogue, Wolfie!' I rolled my eyes up in disapproval. 'Surely she sussed straight away you weren't her granny?'

He lowered his eyes. 'She couldn't see me properly. The afternoon light was fading and the bedroom was steeped in winter gloom. Anyway,' he continued, 'I heard Scarlett take some tentative steps towards the bed, and in moments she was before me looking at me with a puzzled expression. I heard a quiver in her voice.'

'"Granny what's happened to your ears they've grown so big and hairy?"

'Tucking them into my nightcap, I replied, "Sadly, old age doesn't come by itself, dearie, but never mind. All the better to hear you with."

'"Granny," she said, looking closely at me. "How strange your eyes look."

'I answered her in my most reassuring voice. "Ah, Scarlet, darling, am I peering? My eyesight is so poor nowadays. Come nearer, dear, so that I can see you properly. Do you have a basket of food for me?" I began to salivate. "I'm so hungry I could eat a horse." I threw my head back and howled with laughter. Scarlett took a quick step back and gave me a frightened look.

'"Grandmamma,' she exclaimed, "your teeth look so big and sharp!"'

'That was my big moment. One that I completely misjudged, I'm afraid, Lia.'

'Leaping out of bed, I howled, "All the better to eat you up!"'

'Well,' Wolfie huffed, 'you have never seen anyone run so fast or yell louder than she did. "Wait! Wait!" I shouted, bounding after her. 'It was only a joke. I've been a vegetarian for years, honestly!'

Anxiety was obvious in his voice as he relived that scene, so I gently stroked his ears.

* 🌙 *
*

'Wolfie, how could you have been such a dork! Of course, the poor girl wouldn't see the funny side of it. She must have been terrified. You said you were planning to eat her!'

He shook his big head and closed his eyes. 'I agree. I completely misjudged the whole situation. I bitterly regret my stupidity now, but I put it down to starvation and the folly of youth. It could have ended very badly for me. Unfortunately, a woodcutter working in the forest heard Scarlett's screams and came after me in rapid pursuit. I ran for my life! I could feel his hot panting breath on my neck. His blade just a whisper from my jugular.' He gulped.

155

'Oh my gosh, no wonder you're afraid of forests!' I sympathised.

His mouth twisted into a grimace. 'I thought for sure I was a goner … then suddenly, in a flash of blinding white light, everything became suspended. The woodcutter moved in slow motion. I felt myself being lifted from the ground, my paws paddled through thin air, I floated above the scene. The next thing I knew the woodcutter vanished and I landed with a thud on the forest floor – at Aurora's feet!'

'You had a near escape, Wolfie.'

'Yes I did.' He bowed his head. 'Aurora rescued me with her magic.' His eyes took on a faraway look. You should know she was most beautiful back then, Lia. Her long hair hung down to her waist resembling red and gold flickering flames. That day, when she looked down on me with her glittering emerald-green eyes, she spoke kindly.'

'"Tich-tich, Wolf, that was a close one. Luckily for you I was around. Maybe that'll teach you never to play practical jokes on anyone again!"

'I found my voice and answered respectfully, "I've learned my lesson."

'"What shall I do with you?" Her eyes flickered with amusement. I hung my head feeling ashamed. "Come now, surely nothing is so bad that you can't make amends." She lifted my chin and held it, her eyes meeting mine.

"You'd be welcome to stay with me. I could do with a companion. Do say yes. Will you come to live with me?" Taking my answer for granted, she set off without looking back. I followed her, shadowing her through the forest. "We'll make a good match you and I, Wolfie." She glanced back at me. "You'll find I'm always on the side of the underdog."'

Wolfie raised his head, his eyes glowing with pride.

'From that day to this I've been Aurora's "familiar".' He noted my puzzled look. 'That means her guardian spirit,' he explained. 'We've stayed together down through the centuries. She was right. We make a good match. I've guarded her loyally and she's given me love, shelter and a sprinkling of magic.'

'So that's your story!' I laughed. 'Little Red Riding Hood is one of my favourite fairy tales.' It's funny to think I'm here with the Big Bad Wolfie.'

'Hmm...' he said gruffly. 'Yes, that's my story, but enough talk. We should try to rest now. We have a difficult day ahead of us.'

'Where are we headed?'

'At first light, we'll take the trail to the north of the island, to the caves.' A shadow crossed his face. 'Your vision showed Aurora being held in dungeons far below the earth where darkness is the element.'

'I saw it in my vision,' I nodded, hearing the unsteadiness in my voice.

'Yes. You were shown Tyra's kingdom.'

'How will we find where her kingdom is?' I stared at him.

'Again, you need to question your powers.' His eyes sparked. Then his voice grew more patient.

'Lia, you still don't have sufficient belief in yourself. Your magic will guide us to her.'

I chewed my bottom lip. 'Yes. You're absolutely right. Of course, I know I can do this.'

'Good lass. Tomorrow we'll travel to the north of the island. Tyra is hidden there deep in a labyrinth of natural caverns and subterranean caves. We have to be ever watchful and guarded.' His eyes scrutinised mine.

'We are venturing into extremely dangerous territory. You're already aware that Tyra's domain is inhabited by a colony of malignant spirits driven underground for their wickedness.'

Keeping my fears to myself, I said in a voice as steady as I could manage: 'I'm ready.'

Wolfie dug a little hollow in the cold compacted earth and curled his body into it. I lay down beside him, snuggling into his thick fur for warmth, and we settled down for a long night.

Chapter 20

When I awoke I found myself half-buried in a bed of
mouldy leaves. I sat up straining to hear any birdsong.
The forest's silence felt unnatural and ominous. A chill
in the air made me wrap my arms around myself and pull
Aurora's coat over me, shielding myself against a murky
mist which rose from the damp cold earth.

Wolfie stood stiffly, sniffing the air. 'I smell
something rotten.' Making low rumbling growls, his
hackles up, he paced back and forth on the decaying forest
floor.

I sniffed the air. I could smell it, too. At first, I
thought it was the smell of the musty leaves I had been
lying on, but no, it was a putrid odour, like something
decomposing. My eyes darted around. I had a foreboding
sense of something closing in. At first invisible cobweb-
like fingers lightly brushed my face and grazed my hand,
then mischievous spirits showed their forms fleetingly
– aerial creatures, sylphs, wisps, malign apparitions
manifesting themselves momentarily in dark-mauve
vapours before dissolving as shadows into the surrounding
murk. I huddled down, covering my face with my hands
while Wolfie stood by me, statue-like, listening intently.
Then he flinched.

At first, it was no more than a chill in the air and a

cloying fetid odour. Daring to steal a look, I saw a shimmer of mist drifting towards us. Next, a sudden flash of pale silver light illuminated a spectral figure. An ancient crone shrouded in grey, her hood pulled down half hiding her withered face, hovered above us. Her eyes glittered with malice when she spoke in a rasping tone.

'You have come seeking my sister. Well, know this! I will never release her. Her wails feed my soul. I grow stronger as she grows weaker. You will not save her.' Her voiced dripped contempt. 'She will rot in my dungeon, and you girl, spawn of my enemy, you will serve me in my spirit kingdom.'

Her gnarled fingers grasped at my wrist with a grip like cold steel.

Wolfie leapt into action. Pulling his lips back in a snarled warning, he bared yellow fangs and, throwing his head back, eyes closed, he gave voice to a long soulful howl which soared into the forest. In response, amber eyes like flickering flames appeared from the gloomy depths of the tightly knotted web of trees. Wolves emerging from the long shadows stealthily moved towards us. First one wolf then another answered Wolfie's distinctive rallying call until the entire pack filled the air with their spine-tingling chorus. They gathered around, waiting for Wolfie to take his place as their leader, then with slow and deliberate movements they advanced on their prey. Canines bared, necks arched, hackles up, they closed the gap on their quarry. In that moment my spirit was one with them. White-hot energy surged through my whole being. I felt the mighty potency of my magic empower me. Springing to my feet I faced my enemy my voice a ferocious howl.

'Be gone, witch!
You have no power over me!'

She levitated above us, her eyes flashing cruelly.

'You will not win, girl! When next we meet I will have gathered all the forces of hell to defeat you. Then we shall see.' With one final bloodcurdling shriek she evaporated, vanishing into the chill morning air.

When we felt certain she'd gone, the wolves gathered around us showing Wolfie a deeply affectionate greeting. I could see by their friendly cheek rubbing and face licking he was being warmly welcomed by the pack. I realised he had a strong unbreakable bond with his kind. It saddened me to think of him being separated from his family and never reunited with his pack. He had endured the life of a lone wolf until fate threw him together with Aurora.

We spent that day with the wolves in the forest and that night we curled up and slept with them for warmth and safety.

At the first glimmer of light, we set off, the wolves giving us their protection to the edge of the forest. Wolfie bowed his head to them in thanks. As the wolves left us, he quietly watched as, one by one, they melted back into the dappled woodland.

When I stepped out from the forest's gloom, strong sunlight made me blink. We followed a coastal track which broadened into a wider path sloping down to a sandy shoreline.

The witch's terrifying apparition had shaken me to the core. I felt tormented by doubt. How could I, an eleven-year-old girl with little experience in the ways of magic, be

a match for her?

'I'm frightened, Wolfie. I'm not strong enough to take on this challenge.'

'It's true, lass,' he agreed. 'Your magic is still in its early stages but it is extremely potent. I agree you can't do this on your own but, with our combined magic, we can win. The only way she could defeat us is to separate us. Trust me on this. If we stay together, we can succeed.

'I do trust you,' I answered him in a husky voice, hardly able to speak because of the lump in my throat. I felt a huge pang of homesickness. I thought longingly of my mum and my human life in a world unconnected with this mystifying one and wondered if I had made the right choice.

'Of course,' he said, reading my thoughts, 'you always could go home at any time you choose. There would be no shame in it. You just have to wish it hard enough.'

Swallowing hard, I put my arms around his neck and buried my face in his coarse fur.

'No. I'm not going home, Wolfie. I won't let you down. I know we can do this together.'

The tide surged in. Gentle waves washed up delicate pearlescent shells and scattered them like sparkling sequins along the shoreline. I felt soothed by the water lapping around my ankles and the gentle rhythmic percussion of waves. My eyes drifted out to the horizon, searching the ocean for something. But what? Thin branches of driftwood carried by the tide littered the surface of the water. A long gnarled piece floated towards me, bobbing on the surface within my reach. At first glance, it looked ordinary but on closer inspection I noticed a uniqueness in its shape. I stretched out and picked it up, turning it over in my hands. I showed it to Wolfe.

'Look at this beautiful piece of wood. It's been carved and sculpted by the ocean.'

As I held it, I sensed it was meant for me and that somehow it was going to become part of me.

I carried my precious find to the beach and sat cross-legged on the wet, wave-grooved sand. I held the long tapered piece of driftwood in my hand, running my fingers along its grooves and ridges and feeling its energy imbued by the sea. As the waves broke around my feet, I felt its connection to me. It compelled me to use it to write words in the wet sand.

In sunless place she's made to stay.
Now you must wait till end of day,
Night sky her name will point the way.

Wolfie read the message and exclaimed, 'Lia! You've found your wand! It will protect and guide you.' I held it lightly and read out letters carved into the wood:

WVGSJE

'My magic wand's engraved! What does it mean, Wolfie?'

'The letters stand for Wisdom, Victory, Goodness, Success, Justice and Enlightenment. The wand is a magical tool for you to use. It is charged with your energy and is an extension of your power. It belongs to only you and can be used only by you.'

'My own magic wand!' I said, waving it around in the air.

'Beware!' Wolfie barked. 'Lia, you must not use it

frivolously.' He confronted me with a stern look. 'Did you know every act of magic distorts the equilibrium of the world which can have far-reaching consequences? A spell can cause great harm if miscast. You must learn to use your magic with wisdom, thoughtfulness and caution, and only ever to do good.'

'I'm sorry.' I dropped it faster than a red-hot poker. 'Truthfully, I didn't realise having a wand would be such an immense responsibility.'

He shook his head with impatience and, examining my wand more closely, he explained.

'Wands come from many different types of wood, elder, yew, rowan, ash, to name but a few, but yours is from the sequoia tree – the king of trees. The mighty redwood. This wand is truly special and is only given to the most powerful of witches. It will give you strength and protection and will always be your guiding light.'

With his wise words, the incoming tide washed over my sand-written message and dispersed it into the ocean. I placed my precious wand into the satchel, and we hunkered down together in tussocks of long seagrass waiting for nightfall.

Chapter 21

Glad of its warmth, I wrapped Aurora's coat tight round me, hoping that somehow she would know we were coming for her. 'Her name will point the way' – what could that mean? I wondered. The night air held a stillness. We sat together under a clear starry sky, gazing over the glistening sea which mirrored the pale silvery moon. A light wind rippled the surface of the water. I had almost dropped off to sleep when I felt Wolfie stir. He tensed and pricked up his ears.

'What is it, Wolfie?' I jolted alert, looking around.

'Look up, Lia!' His nose pointed to the sky. The air had become charged with magical energy. A faint pearly arc appeared in the sky. I watched in awe as it gradually grew stronger, radiating glowing bands of white light, illuminating the heavens. It gradually grew in intensity, morphing into spectacular ribbons of green, blue and red, dancing across the sky in a harlequin of colours which slowly merged into one other. The sea reflected this spectacular array of colours.

'I've never seen anything so beautiful. What an amazing spectacle!' I gasped in wonder as the sky undulated and rippled above us. 'What is it?' I breathed.

'They call it the Aurora Borealis, or "The Merry Dancers",' Wolfie whispered.

'The universe has sent a solar wind to bring us a message.'

The lights danced between the stars, and as we sat mesmerised they merged into one singular finger of tapering green light, pointing downwards – it hung above the huge fearsome rock formation silhouetted black against the night sky. 'Wolfie, do you see? It's showing us where Aurora is! It's pointing the way!'

'The Aurora! Of course! Her name! We've found her.'

At first light, we forged ahead, following the coastal track towards the crags. The morning star winked down on us as we picked our way carefully through mounds of seagrass alive with small brown frogs leaping around our feet. After the long cold night, daybreak brought a glimmer of warmth.

As the coastline curved round, the vast and fearful wind-worn rock came into view. It rose steeply, its grey pitted face gashed with jagged crevices that gave it the look of an angry giant. Biting wind whipped around us as we continued our way along the coastal path. Eventually, we were led down to a strip of black pebble beach where the base of the rock met the ocean. I kicked off my shoes and walked along the beach, the sharp stones and pebbles pushing into my soles.

'How on earth will we find the way in?' I stared up at the cliff face rising sharply behind us.

Wolfie, intent in sniffing around a rocky outcrop didn't reply.

As I clambered over to join him, I noticed the glint of something half-submerged in a rockpool. Reaching down I cupped my hands and scooped up a small blue glass bottle. Its opaque colour reminded me of the bottles Aurora

169

used to store her spells. Brushing sand from its smooth sides, I held it up to the light and detected something inside. I prised the stopper from its neck and fished out a tightly rolled scrap of paper. It was another message in riddle form for us:

*A twisting path to giant weeping
Will take you to the one you're seeking.
An upward climb and then a fall,
And drop of water will show you all.
Behind cascade you'll find the portal,
An entrance hidden from
Wolf and Mortal.*

We headed up to the base of the cliff where we sheltered from the wind in a little cove. Flashes of white water bounced down the rock face, gushing into the foaming waves bellow. I looked up, trying to pinpoint the source of the tumbling water.

'Wolfie! I've figured out the message!' I pointed up.

'Behind cascade you'll find the portal! The way in is behind the mouth of a waterfall!'

While I was speaking a beautiful shimmering blueish-green dragonfly alighted on my shoulder. It rested there for one brief moment before hovering overhead. A ray of sun captured its iridescent wings making them glint like sapphires.

'A dragonfly is a good omen,' Wolfie assured me. 'It's well known that it symbolises a change for the good.'

The dragonfly fluttered above us and seemed to beckon us to follow it up a steep path towards the waterfall. I scrambled up the rock face, gripping on to the tough leathery grasses and grabbing on to small bushes which

helped pull me up through the steep, difficult climb.

Wolfie sure-footedly took the climb easily. Racing ahead of me, from time to time he stood patiently on a narrow ledge, waiting for me to catch up. Reaching for another handhold I pulled myself up and carefully edged my way along crumbling narrow ledges, all the while avoiding looking down at the sheer drop below. The deafening down-rush of water told us we were nearing the waterfall. As we approached, the water's roar became deafening, the force of its spray drenching us.

Behind the iron-grey torrent, we could see the gaping mouth of a cave. With a shudder I thought: this is the entrance to Tyra's underworld! With a pounding heart, I clung on to the wet slippery moss-covered sides of the cliff face, and, still led by the dragonfly, we inched our way behind the curtain of thundering water. As we passed through the cave's dark entrance, the sight inside made me gawp in amazement.

'It's so incredibly beautiful,' I gasped. The cave walls glowed and glittered in red, orange and rich gold hues. I reached out to touch its jewel-like surface.

'Careful!' shouted Wolfie over the din of crashing water. 'Touch it at your peril! The red stones are cinnabar, the gold arsenopyrite, and the orange orpiment – all deadly poisonous!'

I quickly withdrew my hand, understanding now that we were in a very dangerous place. As we moved into the inner cave, I felt waves of panic. I strained my eyes to see through the inky blackness, and as we ventured further into the cave's interior, the weak light cast by the dragonfly illuminated a wraithlike figure slowly floating towards us.

I shrank into the shadows as it came nearer, then, with a jolt, I saw her clearly, momentarily lit in thin ghostly light. Aurora!

She held her arms open to me and spoke in a piteous voice.

'Lia, please follow me.'

I took a quick step towards her. 'Aurora. Wait!' I called to her.'

She pressed a finger to her lips before vanishing down a dark cold passageway.

'We have to follow her,' I whispered to Wolfie, my hand reaching out for him in the dark, but he was gone.

'Wolfie!' I called into the darkness. 'Come to me. I'm scared. Where are you?' I inched further into the cave, afraid to feel my way along wet slimy walls. 'Wolfie. Please come back. Where are you?' I called again this time with a note of desperation in my voice.

The only sound that came back was my own shaky voice echoing through the cave chambers. Had Wolfie followed Aurora? No, I scolded myself. He would never abandon me like that. Stumbling through the dark cave, I called out his name and in my panic I tripped on the uneven surface of the cave floor and fell heavily, grazing my knee.

'I can't do this on my own,' I choked, sitting where I'd fallen, holding my head in my hands, very close to tears.

A slight whirring noise by my ear made me look up. The dragonfly was still with me. It hung over me, beating its wings in agitation, then, still quivering in front of me, it morphed into a tiny luminous fairy. I blinked as it cast a soft halo of light around us. The fairy spoke in a peeved, tinkling voice.

'I'm putting myself in danger here just to guide you, mortal, so the least you can do is stand up and follow me. Your kind isn't trusted by faerie folk.' She added in a scathing voice.

'I don't understand,' I ventured timidly.

In a bitter tone she scolded, 'Perhaps if you were to stop harming Mother Earth we would think more kindly of your race.' She beat her tiny transparent wings in anger, but then she said in a slightly kinder tone 'I am told you have come to seek our friend, and I have been sent to help you.'

'You're wrong,' I proclaimed. 'I'm not a mortal! I am Vanilia Solveig, and I care passionately about protecting the Earth.'

'Ah.' she nodded 'So you are the one! From the Wind, the Sea and the House of Strength. I understand now why I have been sent to guide you. You are the great and powerful witch my people have been waiting for. Huh!' She gave me a look filled with scorn. 'You are no powerful witch! You are just a child! Come with me, girl!'

'I can't come alone,' I stuttered. 'I have to wait here for Wolfie. I'm sure he'll come back for me.'

The fairy spoke in a sharp tone. 'The wolf cannot come back for you. The witch has snatched and enfeebled him. She is afraid of your combined magic. She thinks by separating you she will conquer you. She has ensnared the wolf using dark magic. It was not Aurora you saw drawing you forward; it was an illusion of her sent to distract you. The wolf can't help you now, but' – her voice softened – 'there are others who can.'

'Who can help me?' I questioned her suspiciously, recalling Wolfie's words.

'Beware of the faerie folk. Some will fool you, some will lure you into danger. Some will wish to bring you harm.'

'So how do I know I can trust you?' I narrowed my

eyes, fighting to keep my voice steady.

'You don't,' she answered in a voice as cold as the North Wind, 'but you have no choice.'

The faerie buzzed in a frenzy around my head. 'You are in the very heart of Tyra's kingdom. This is where she wields her greatest power. You are in great danger. Do you understand why?' She beat her wings in my face. 'She fears you and knows you are close to succeeding in your quest. She is afraid your magic combined with the witch Aurora's and the wolf's will prove so powerful you will overcome her. You must follow me now. It is not safe for you to linger here. Come.' Not waiting for my reply, she flew before me, illuminating the way as she bathed the cavern in a subdued orange glow.

Her flickering light led me through a series of small dark caves into narrow passageways. Rough steps hewn into the rock led us down and downwards through dark shadowy corridors, further and further, deeper and deeper, into the bowels of the Earth. As we descended I could hear the faint sound of distant rushing water.

Chapter 22

It felt scary emerging from the narrow passageway's stale air into a huge cavern lit by burning torches. Am I expected? I thought with a shudder. When I had grown accustomed to the subdued light, my eyes were drawn to the source of running water. An underground river twisted its way through the cave's labyrinths. A small boat made of driftwood bobbed at the water's edge.

The little fairy spoke in her tinkling voice. 'I have to leave you here. My task is done.'

And with a flutter of her wings, she morphed back into a dragonfly and was gone.

I fought down rising panic, reminding myself I wasn't alone. She'd promised me benevolent forces were watching over me. Feeling comforted by that thought, I cast my eye around the cave wondering which way to go when a rustling noise above me made me glance up. The cave's roof seemed to be shifting and moving. A high-pitched screeching noise shattered the silence making me cover my ears and in that moment the cave came to life with a flurry of hundreds of bats diving and swooping around my head. I threw my hands up to protect my head and ran for cover when the bats descended on me flapping their wings threateningly, clawing at my hair. Make for the river! Just get out of here, I thought. Without further delay,

I clambered into the boat and pushed it away from the side. My heart pounded in my ears as I rowed hard into the river's current, propelling the small vessel into a wide dark tunnel carved through the rock.

It felt safer to curl up tight, huddling myself into a ball on the floor of the boat until I was sure I'd safely left the swarming bats behind. Rippling water cast mystical reflections on the tunnel's roof as the swell of the river pushed the fragile boat on. The fast-flowing water forced the boat into a narrower channel where a sudden powerful surge pitched the little vessel into a precariously chaotic path. Even huddled down, I got soaked in spray as strong currents buffeted and tossed the little craft up and down white foaming rapids. Powerful turbulence dashed the boat against the sides of the tunnel, almost capsizing it. My muffled cries were drowned by the roar of rushing water. With eyes scrunched tight shut, terrified of capsizing, I gripped the sides of the boat, holding on with grim determination. The little boat whooshed around a wide bend where the current thankfully slowed and the water became placid again. My small cry of relief echoed when the little vessel steadied and righted itself. From that point, the river wound swiftly and smoothly through shadowy passageways until it emerged from the mouth of the tunnel, catapulting the boat into a limpid rock pool its luminescence resembling a sea of stars. Hundreds of luminous blue glow-worms, suspended from the grotto's ceiling, glowed and glittered and were mirrored and reflected in the pool's electric-blue water.

My wobbly legs barely supported me as I clambered out of the boat, scouting around to get my bearings. The grotto formed part of a labyrinth of interconnecting caves and passageways branching out in

diverse directions. Which way should I go? The absolute silence – apart from the sound of my footsteps – made me feel utterly lost and alone.

'Aurora, if you can reach out to me, please give me a sign,' I murmured aloud.

Hardly able to believe my ears, I heard from far off faint strains of fiddle music playing. I recognised the tune: 'The Stars Align,' the very first piece of music I'd heard Aurora play. It must be a sign. Could she be using music to guide me to her? I followed the twinkling blue glow-worms' light trail through the maze of caves, a magnetic energy-force drawing me on through this unearthly world of dark spaces. The light petered out, and the twisting uneven path ended abruptly in a suffocatingly airless chamber.

I realised with dread that this must be the threshold of Tyra's inner sanctum. Peering into the darkness, I could just make out a heavy iron-bound door set into the rock. The symbol of an eye carved into the door glared down at me alongside the words 'I SEE ALL.' My spine tingled with fear as I gripped the heavy door knocker, striking it three times. The loud bangs reverberated and echoed into the silence. My rapid breathing was the only sound to break the silence until a sinister breathy voice hissed from the shadows:

COME FORTH!

As the heavy door creaked and scraped open, a

freezing blast hit me. A wondrous sight met my eyes as I stepped into the enormous cavern. Wow! I stared up in amazement at its spectacular domed roof supported by magnificent columns of ice-carved stalactites hanging down from the ceiling and stalagmites rising to meet them. The music drew me into this surreal landscape. Beautiful intricate rainbow-coloured rock formations grew from the walls like a hanging garden. Tiny lights danced across the walls, sprinkling the floor with reflected rainbows from ice crystal-encrusted walls, their magnificence dazzling me so completely that I momentarily forget my fear. From high above, a speck of light penetrated the darkness, spotlighting a frozen lake smooth as black polished glass and edged in thin sheets of undulated rock resembling heavy draped black curtains.

The temperature dropped to below freezing, making me shiver with both cold and fear. The atmosphere become laden with menace. The hairs on the back of my neck prickled. Something malevolent was coming. Breaking into a cold sweat I tried to run, but a column of sulphurous foul-smelling mist rose from the ground and began stealthily snaking its way up and around my throat making me gag and choke. Fear made me stagger backwards, and losing my footing I fell heavily to the ground. The music which had drawn me on grew louder and closer and now I could see its source. Half-hidden by shadow, a dark demonic figure came swaying towards me. A harbinger of evil, it played increasingly high-pitched frenzied music paving the way for its mistress's entrance. Powerless to move, I lay helpless while an odour of rot and decay announced Tyra's presence. Her disembodied, rasping voice rang out.

'You have been deceived, witch.' She laughed cruelly. 'My Fossegrimen's music has lured you here. You are now entrapped.' She screamed a command at the creature. 'Seize her!'

Quickly, think! Jolted into action by her threat, I scrambled to my feet and, pulling my satchel open, I grasped my wand in my trembling hand.

The wand sprung to life, growing into a strong sturdy staff. It beat out mercilessly at the creature until, overcome, the Fossegrimen dissolved back into the shadows. Galvanised by fear, I cast around searching frantically for an escape from this hideous place. My eyes swept the far side of the frozen lake, catching sight of a deep cave embedded in the glacier wall. Glistening black ice crystals had been magically elongated over its entrance to form prison bars. My mouth felt dry. I felt certain this ice-cave had been shown to me in the image at the well, I understood that it was here where Aurora and Wolfie were imprisoned. I scrambled to my feet. Spurred on by a huge rush of fear and the need to get to them I followed the path around the lake and as I drew nearer to the cave-prison embedded in the wall an appalling sight made my blood run cold. Through black translucent ice, I glimpsed the faint outline of Aurora reaching out towards Wolfie. Both were trapped inside the glacier, frozen in ice, suspended in time, just as it had been shown to me in my vision. Their frozen figures stared down at me.

Hoping that somehow I could still communicate with them, I gazed up at their motionless figures and, reaching out to them, I said forcefully, 'I've come to set you free.'

My inner voice spoke urgently to me: Consult the spell book. Maybe I would find an incantation in it to strengthen my magic. A dark shadowy corner hidden out of sight proved the perfect place to conceal myself, and pulling the spell book from my satchel I began to study it, pouring over it until my head hurt, but still I struggled to make any sense of any of it.

'It's hopeless.' I rubbed my temples and laid the book aside. Out of nowhere, a hoarse, gravelly voice spoke to me:

'Aye, I see you've finally got around to putting some faith in me.'

My eyes darted around, looking for whoever had spoken, hoping someone had come to help me, but I saw nobody.

'Righty-o. I hope I'm not rusty, I haven't been consulted in a while,' the voice continued in an accusing tone. 'Let me teach you how to go about properly casting a spell.'

With a shock I realised that the spell book was speaking to me and in a Scots accent! Why should I be surprised? Now that it had my full attention, the disembodied voice continued:

'Good. At last we have a connection. I get the feeling you're nervous and stressing about the fine details?'

'You're absolutely right,' I agreed. 'I can't make sense of the script and symbols,' I explained, slightly bewildered by the idea of speaking to a book!

'No need to overthink it,' the voice said in a relaxed tone. 'If you stumble over a few incantations or forget what you were supposed to say, it isn't going to be an earth-shattering mistake. Deep down you already know what to do, don't you? You are not a complete beginner. Aurora has already taught you – it's your intent that matters. You have to focus absolutely on your intent.'

'Intent. Yes, I do understand that,' I replied, 'and I've already had a little success in my spell making.'

'Good,' the voice continued. 'I know it can seem overwhelming but don't waste time worrying that it's not going to work. If you spend time doubting yourself, it could interfere with your magic. When you cast a spell, you're saying words which help move energy in the direction of your intention. Your energy is coupled with your intent and willpower, which makes your spell more potent. In the grand scheme of things, every step of a spell is simply a way to solidify your intention and channel your energy.'

'By my intent, you mean whatever it is I desire.' I leaned over the book, studying it.

'Exactly! As long as you stay focused and allow yourself time to get into the right mindset – how would you say it nowadays? – get into the zone, you won't fail. Now, if you feel ready, shall we begin?'

Chapter 23

'Please open me at Chapter 3 and consult my wisdom.'

'"Chapter 3: The First Basic Principles of Spell Casting." Yes I've found it.'

I began to read. 'First, you must choose a space suitably large enough to cast a circle.' I looked around and spied the perfect place. A large secluded alcove recessed into the rock. It would also make a good hiding place.

'The circle is for your protection, Lia. It has to be wide enough for you to stand in its centre.'

Preparing to draw out my circle in the soft earth, I was about to use the point of my crystal when the spell book interrupted me.

'Before you step into the circle you must gather a simple representation of the four elements: Earth, Air, Fire and Water.'

I'll never be sure if it was inner magic or just a brilliant flash of inspiration but I knew exactly where I could find those elements. The satchel held the gifts from the women on Sileby Island. I visualised its contents: the crystals, the bag of pungent-smelling herbs, a pebble, a shell, two candles and feathers. I lifted out the pebble to represent Earth, the feather to represent Air, the candle to represent Fire, and I used the shell to scoop up melted ice to represent Water. I gathered all my elements together and began drawing out my circle, all the while consulting the pages of the spell book for guidance.

It counselled me: 'Don't forget to step into your circle before you close it!'

'Good. Well done. Now connect the line of the circle. Like closing a door, you will be protected inside. Excellent. Now mark out the points of a compass in your circle: North, East, South and West. Place your representations from the four elements at each corresponding point of the compass. Excellent. Now please meditate on these words.

From east to south and north to west,
guided by spirits manifest,
I call Mother Nature to attend,
together to help me to this end.
With good intent and hands steadfast,
within the circle rightly cast,
safe from hex or curse or blast
I trust in you and cast my spell.
Your favours I will honour well,
From cave and desert, hill and sea,
I call you now ¬ attend on me
THIS IS MY WILL SO MOTE IT BE!

Making sure I took the spell book with me, I stood in the centre of the circle.

It is crucial,' it warned, 'that you do not pass out of the circle lest you weaken the magic. Now you must get in tune with the elements. Stand in the centre of the circle facing east and imagine the wind whipping around you:

Spirit of Air, I call upon you!

188

'Now stand facing west and imagine water flowing around you:

Spirit of Water. I call upon you!

'Now stand facing south and feel the sun's energy giving life to the Earth:

Spirit of Fire, I call upon you!

'Now stand facing north and feel your feet rooted and drawn deep to the core of the Earth:

Spirit of Earth, I call upon you.

'Now still facing north and visualise bringing radiant white light from the centre of the Earth up into your being:

Mother Earth, I call upon you!

'Next, send a column of light up from the crown of your head out of the Earth's atmosphere into the cosmos. Bring golden-white light from the cosmos down into your being and say:

Father Earth, I call upon you!

'You may now work your magic, but first, thank the elements for their intervention. Focus the energy you've raised and merge it with your intent. This is the moment to believe in yourself Lia and proclaim your desire.'

Yes, I felt certain I'd followed each instruction to the letter. The speck of light penetrating the cavern's ceiling shifted its beam until it shone directly above me suffusing me with energy. It coursed through my body, giving me a thrilling feeling of exhilaration. Closing my eyes, I trusted completely in myself focusing on one thought only. I entreated the spirits to give me the power to free Aurora and Wolfie. Raising my eyes to the intense source of light, I seized on its dynamic energy-force channelling and directing it to do my will.

The dazzling beam of light widened and strengthened. It cast around the cavern like a searchlight, alighting on little pockets of methane gas leaking out from crevices in the rock. Hot air circulated and intensified the heat, causing pockets of gas to ignite. They spluttered into tongues of flame which leapt high and licked the cave walls. The temperature soared. The ice melted gushing in rivulets into the lake. The glacier imprisoning Aurora and Wolfie gave way in a torrent of black foetid meltwater.

'It is done.' The spell book's voice resounded around the cave. 'They are free.'

I bowed my head and spoke my concluding words:

The circle is open but can never be broken.

'I've done it!' I exhaled a long breath and unclenched my fists.

Aurora stood swaying on her feet, rubbing her eyes, as if coming out of a deep sleep.

Wolfie stood alongside her, his tail down, his eyelids drooping. I ran to them and fell to my knees. Wrapping my arms around Wolfie's neck, I buried my face in his coarse fur.

'Wolfie!' I choked back tears. The corners of his

mouth twitched up, and he gave my face a warm lick. Aurora laid a light hand on my shoulder. 'I knew you would come.'

She stood calm and dignified, smiling her special smile, resplendent in a halo of white shimmering light.

'Come!' she beckoned me.' Follow me. We must leave this wicked place at once.' As she whirled around a bloodcurdling scream stopped her in her tracks. Aurora gripped my hand in hers and mouthed, 'Tyra!'

The atmosphere became charged with danger. A foul odour of decay permeated every corner of the cave heralding her presence. Her disembodied voice boomed out like a rising storm.

'You are exactly where I want you now, Aurora.' She gave a bitter laugh. 'The witch, her cur and the girl you have beguiled. You three will never leave my kingdom. You will remain here for eternity and be my slaves.'

Chapter 24

The lake's surface rippled and shifted, radiating a glow
that illuminated the cavern in green ghostly light. Its centre
began to seethe and boil, and with a huge eruption a gush
of vile slimy effluence threw up a hideous snake-like
creature, dark green in colour and flashing yellow glowing
eyes. It rose from the depths of the lake with a hideous
shriek and levitated above the dark swirling waters, hissing
menacingly.

Aurora took a decisive step forward and spoke out,
her voice filled with contempt.

'So this is how you manifest yourself, Tyra. As a
base, slithering serpent. Aye, it is apt as you are indeed a
venomous creature.' She raised her voice higher. 'I have
no fear of you. Your influence is no more, your sovereignty
over. Your magic is diminishing, your powers grow ever
weaker.' She gave a mirthless laugh. 'By bringing us three
together you sought to plunder our energy to refuel and
strengthen your own.' Her eyes blazing, she continued in a
withering tone: 'You have not succeeded.'

The creature spat and writhed. Contorting its jaw, it
flicked its forked tongue and drawing back black lips over
dripping fangs it hissed, 'A hex on you, Aurora. I curse
you.'

Aurora's eyes flashed in anger and in a scathing

tone she countered: 'You failed to heed the code by which we strive to live and practice our magic, Tyra.

As yea harm none, do what yea will.

Her features clouded as she stretched out her hands.
'Tyra, you have saddened me more than I can say. We were sisters who once loved each other. I would never wish to harm you, but' – her face hardened – 'through your wickedness, you, and you alone, are the architect of your downfall.'

She took a small step back and taking my hand in hers she placed her other hand on Wolfie's head. Her voice rang out clear and steadfast.

'You brought us three together thinking you would steal our powers, but you forgot! Uniting us, you have strengthened our power threefold!'

Her voice reverberated around the caves.

'Now you must bear the consequences of your evil.'

Spreading her arms out, she raised her eyes:

I invoke the power of three –
what thou send out comes back to thee.
See the cruelty and the pain
that you have caused time and again.
I turn the tables three by three –
hear my voice I will be free!
When light fades and dark comes
through
the pain you've caused comes back to you!
This spell I've made in karma tonight,
I am a witch I stand and fight!

Ever mind the rule of three:
three times your act return to thee.
The lesson now that must be learned:
Thou will get back what thou hast
earned.

A blinding flash illuminating a great bellow of water made me shrink back and cover my eyes with my hands to protect them. The geyser erupted from the boiling lake and showered us in scalding droplets.

Aurora pushed me behind her to shield me. Wolfie launched himself at the lake.

'Stay!' Aurora commanded but he refused to be held back.

I cowered behind her, stealing frightened glances at the creature thrashing around in the water venting its wrath. The temperature plummeted to a bone-rattling cold. The lake seethed in turmoil. Its churning currents twisted, swirled, whirled around and around, spinning faster and faster, creating an awesome whirlpool. Its gathering momentum transformed it into a monster maelstrom. I recoiled in horror, burying my face in my hands as the mighty vortex relentlessly sucked the reptilian creature down into its centre. After one final ferocious lash from her spiked tail the creature gave an anguished wail as the swirling water roiled around her and swallowed her into its core, devouring her.

Aurora's arms dropped to her side. The lake's surface stilled and once more became as smooth as glass.

'Is it over?' I whispered hardly daring to look.

Aurora turned to me her eyes glistening. 'Aye.' She wiped at her eyes. 'It's over but it was not a sweet victory.' She placed a hand on my shoulder. 'Come on, lass. Let's go home.'

When the murk settled I looked for Wolfie and sighted him lying in a crumpled heap at the edge of the lake. I ran to him and dropped to my knees, cradling his big head in my lap. He lay cold and unmoving. My heart lurched in fear.

'Aurora,' I choked, 'I think Wolfie's been badly hurt.' I watched the colour drain from her face as she gazed down at his lifeless form.

'Is he breathing?' she whispered in a barely audible voice. 'Oh, the poor lad. Has he given up his life to protect us?'

'No! 'I said in a tremulous voice. 'That can't be!' I hugged him to me, burying my face in his fur. 'Don't die, Wolfie!'

Aurora picked up the satchel and dropped down on her knees beside him.

'We have to do something!' she said in a determined voice, rifling through the bag.

'Malachite, a candle, a crystal, ah!' Relief showed in her face 'Thank goodness, a healing spell.' She took the little glass jar from the satchel and cupped it in her hands. As she leaned over it, I saw its white glow brighten to a strong powerful light which reflected and flared in her eyes. Placing a shaky hand first on Wolfie's head then running it down the length of his back, she spoke in earnest:

Heal what has been hurt,
change the fates design
Save what has been lost
bring back what is mine.
With this healing light
Help us in our plight.

Cradling Wolfie in my arms, I fought down rising panic.

'Please, Wolfie, don't die,' I whispered in his ear, holding him close.

With a surge of hope I felt him twitch slightly and give a small whine.

'Aurora, he's alive!'

She gave me a small nod and continued running her hand down his back speaking to him in a gentle voice.

'There there, Wolfie, my brave lad. Lie quietly until you feel recovered.'

Wolfie merely gave a feeble wave of his tail.

We sat with him awhile until he rallied.

'Wolfie, do you feel strong enough to travel?' Aurora questioned him.

'Yes. I feel much stronger now. Let's waste no more time and be on our way.' He struggled up on shaky legs. 'It will be good to leave this accursed place. Are we travelling back via Eynenholm?'

She nodded. 'Yes. They're waiting for me. They need me there. There is much we have to discuss. What do you say, Lia?' She levelled a questioning look at me. 'Will we pay them a visit them on our way home?'

'Yes. I would like to see them,' I agreed, feeling excited to be seeing Megan again. 'As time isn't of any consequence here, I guess there's no reason why we shouldn't drop in for a quick visit before we go home.'

Aurora rubbed her hands together. 'Good, then it's decided. I will summon a spell to transport us.'

'Naw,' Wolfie shook his head emphatically. 'No more of your unreliable spells of transportation, Aurora! The old ways are best.'

'You are right, old friend.' She smiled, glad to see his feisty spirit restored. 'I am a silly old woman! In the future I will think long and hard before dabbling in the new ways. My foolish vanity put me in danger and not only me, but you too. Thank you, Wolfie. I am well advised to stick to what I know.'

He nodded, relieved.

'Very well.' She pulled herself up straight. 'I'll summon the besom.' Closing her eyes, she snapped her fingers. In an instant the broomstick buzzed around us, coming to rest at her feet.

'But can we all fit on to it?' I had my doubts.

'Certainly!' She tapped a finger on the broomstick. 'My besom is very strong and accommodating.' With that the broomstick obliged her by widening and lengthening.

'You see, Wolfie.' She gave him a sideways look. 'The besom does as it is bid sometimes.'

'Aye,' he snorted, 'when it feels like it. Do you know what the scallywag did? It …'

Aurora threw her hands up. 'I'm not listening to any tales!' She opened her satchel and began examining its contents. 'Do I have everything I need?' She pulled items from the bag checking them off. My compass for direction, yes, my herbs, yes – chamomile for luck and bay leaf for protection. Perfect!' She gave a slight nod. 'Oh good, and a candle to light our way.'

She sat cross-legged, organising each item on the ground in front of her, and when she felt satisfied she held her hands quite still above the broomstick and murmured:

By light of stars and Lady Moon
we'll reach our destination soon.
Our trip will safe and happy be,
for all concerned as well as me.
Through dark night sky
our way will wend,
bear us steadfast to journey's end.

Placing everything back in the satchel, she declared herself ready to go. Wolfie stealthily crept up behind the broomstick and without warning pinned it down with his big paw.

Breathing heavily, he gave it a hard stare. 'No more of your blasted nonsense, ye wee wretch,' he growled.

'Your mission is to carry us to Eynenholm.' He took the broomstick in his jaws and gave it a shake for good measure before dropping it unceremoniously to the ground. The broomstick swished back and forth, furious at this slight to its dignity.

Aurora's eyes twinkled. 'Do not be mistaken, Lia, those two may appear to be at odds but they are allies and have my best interests at heart.' She turned to them and in a stern voice chided, 'Now, enough of this bickering, you two. Are we ready for take-off?'

We all climbed on to the broomstick and held on tight. Raising her eyes upwards, Aurora focused on the speck of light beaming down on us from the chink in the cave's roof. It expanded and widened into a brilliant shaft, spilling golden rays down over us. A warm zephyr wind blew around us, wafting us upwards, higher and higher towards the light's source. The chink opened wide to allow us to pass through, and I gave a great whoop as we burst out and flew into the rosy dawn.

Chapter 25

It felt good to have cool fresh air rush by as we climbed higher and higher through a bright morning sky. As the evening star faded, we flew onwards through wispy white clouds. The broomstick headed south. After the oppressive gloominess in the caves, the landscape spread out below us appeared vibrant and vivid. The bright morning sunshine lifted my spirits.

'We'll steer a course south-east and head towards the coast.' Aurora directed the broomstick, causing it to accelerate and veer to the right.

We flew above towering red cliffs buttressing a sparkling blue ocean. As we cruised along at a steady altitude, Aurora cheerfully shouted behind her through the whistling wind. 'A guid day for flying, is it no'?' I glanced back. A witch on her broomstick, her cloak billowing around her, flew alongside us. She clutched on to her hat as she shouted a greeting.

'Good day, Dame Aurora. You are indeed a sight for sore eyes. I have been despatched to find you.'

'Good day to you, Dame Sybil. I am sorry I have vexed everyone. I know I am a wee bit late, but alas,' – she forced a smile – 'I was waylaid. No matter. By hook or by crook I will arrive presently.'

Steadying her broomstick, the witch replied. 'I am

happy to find you safe, dear friend. I'll fly ahead to give the others the good news.'

Aurora thanked her, adding, 'Aye. Tell them we will shortly be gathered together with one more than usual added to our baker's dozen.'

'Fare thee well.' Sybil waved us goodbye. 'Until we meet at …'

She took off at high speed leaving nothing but a trail of shimmering light particles in her wake, her words lost in the blustering wind.

'How much further?' I hollered into the wind. Aurora pointed into the distance to the grey outline of Sileby Castle and shouted, 'We're nearly there … Look, you can see the tower.' We picked up the pace, flying over rough grazing land bordering yellow-and-brown striped fields.

'Hold on, we're going down.! Aurora yelled, bending her head into the wind.

The broomstick suddenly nose-dived, and plummeting down it came to a skidding, juddering halt as we landed with a thud in the middle of a field of cows. I catapulted off landing on all fours, narrowly missing a cow pat. Aurora helped me to my feet and brushed me down.

'Oh, my stars! That gleckit besom. Are you hurt, Lia?'

'No, I'm OK.'

'Be off with you, scallywag,' she told the broomstick.

Wolfie nodded his resounding approval at the broomstick's banishment.

'Don't worry, Lia dear,' Aurora assured me. 'I can always rely on the besom to come back to me.'

'Hmphhhh,' Wolfie snorted.

'Now let's hurry. As you know, if the tide comes in, access to the castle will become submerged. We put on a spurt and reached the castle as the afternoon gave way to dusk. We passed through the keep's massive entrance door and were met in the Great Hall by Dame Sybil.

'Aurora!' she cried, her whole face lighting up. 'You are safe.'

The other women gathered around, and taking her into their midst they swept her into a group hug.

Megan came towards me, a worried expression on her face. 'I'm relieved you're back safe, Lia.' Her forehead furrowed. 'We were all worried about you.'

'I'm glad to see you again, Megan.' I hugged her. 'I've loads to tell you. It's difficult to know where to begin.'

She hooked her arm through mine and led me over to a high-backed bench in the inglenook corner of the fire.

'Let's build up a blaze.'

She handed me logs from a basket, and I helped throw them onto the crackling fire.

When we were cosily settled, she tucked a stray lock of hair behind her ear and, fixing inquisitive eyes on me, urged, 'Tell me everything!'

I began relating our adventure to Megan, her eyes growing wide when I described our nightmarish encounters with Tyra. Bombarding me with questions, she listened to my answers agog. Pressing a hand to her cheek, she exclaimed, 'You didn't run from her. You didn't back down! You've been so brave.'

Wolfie, who was stretched out sleeping on the hearth at our feet, yelped and whimpered in his sleep.

Soon huge trays of food were being carried in from the kitchen. A feast! Meats, cheeses, bannocks, loaves of bread, fruits, cakes, sweets, puddings and huge jugs of cordial and heather ale.

Megan jumped up. 'Come on, let's eat!'

201

Helping me to some little sugared crescent-moon shaped biscuits, she said in an excited voice, 'I can't wait!' She jiggled her foot. 'After we've eaten and the speechifying's over, we're all going down to the beach. We've made a fire pit. It'll be brilliant fun! We'll sit around the blaze telling stories, singing and playing music. I hope you're not too tired?' Her cat's eyes glinted. 'We can stay up until the wee small hours of the morning.'

'I don't feel in the least tired. Bring it on!' I laughed, thinking, I like her. She's so funny and I can be myself with her. She makes me feel comfortable. I relaxed into the happy party atmosphere, appreciating the warm feeling of friendship around the table.

'Have some more.' Megan offered me a slice of frosted snow cake.

'No, honestly I can't. I'm stuffed.' I groaned, holding my stomach.

'Go on!' she laughed, tipping it on to my plate.

Although I hadn't known her for long, I knew for sure we had made a lasting friendship.

Aurora rose from her seat and tapped her fingers on the table.

'I will keep this brief.' The corners of her mouth twitched up. 'I know the younger ones are keen to get out to the bonfire. As you know dear friends, Ostara is a time of new beginnings, so it is a good time to make our pledges.' She lifted her notes. 'We reflect on our hopes and the good deeds we will do for the coming year. Our work is important.' She adjusted her spectacles and cast an eye around the table, singling me out with her eyes. 'Our planet is fragile and beautiful. It is also small and vulnerable. Do not tolerate injustice to our Earth. Become its protector and a defender of the land, the waters, the trees, the melting ice caps, the ozone layer and endangered species. Focus on the things you can do for the Earth and share those thoughts with others. Spread goodness to increase goodness. We must blaze a trail for those who come after us and never give up! Thank you, everyone.' She laid her notes aside. 'If we're finished around the table let's all go out and light the bonfire.'

'Yaaaay! Come on!' Megan dragged me down the stone stairwell and out down to the beach. 'I'll teach you to change yourself into a cat. It's called transmogrification or, as I say it – trans-moggie-frication!'

I laughed at her joke as we linked arms and made our way down to the firepit where we hunkered down with the others. What a brilliant night! We sang and played music and played games. We formed a circle and danced and sang around the blaze the backdrop of Sileby Castle rising out of the darkness.

When the sun rose to spatter the sky with golden flecks Megan pulled me up from the sand shouting, 'Hey, Lia! It's a new day. New possibilities. Come on!'

Grabbing my hand she pulled me down the beach, and whooping and laughing we splashed into the sea. The freezing water shocked us wide awake. As we paddled through the shallows, I saw her smile fade.

'What's wrong, Megan?' I asked.
'I'm missing my family. It's time I went home.' She dragged her feet through the water.

'Me too,' I replied, realising I felt a terrible yearning that must be homesickness. I missed Mum and had a powerful longing to see her.

Standing by herself at the edge of the sea, Megan lifted her hand in farewell. 'See you!' she called and glancing my way one last time she dropped her arms to her sides and raised her face to the fiery red sun. Her absolute stillness gave me the impression she'd turned into a statue cast in crimson.

'When will I see you again?' I called, but in that instant she vanished.

To distract myself from my feelings of sadness at her leaving, I stayed on the beach awhile. Everyone else had gone up to the castle but I had a lot to think about. Mum would be heading home soon from her work-trip, and it was time I was going home too. When Aurora and Wolfie come down, I thought, I'd say I'm ready to go home now. Digging my toes into the soft sand, I flopped down beside the smouldering fire embers. The dry sticks I threw on for kindling caught the flames and I poked it into life. The fire crackled and a breeze fanned the flames, changing their colour from blue, to purple, to orange and then to red. Deep in the fire's core a picture began to take shape, mesmerising me. The colours mingled and merged, forming an image. When I leaned in to take a closer look I saw it resembled the appearance of a burning plane spiralling down in a plume of black smoke. The wind changed at that point, making the fire splutter and sending out a shower of scorching red and yellow sparks. I jerked back and covered my stinging eyes from the noxious fumes. Stumbling up, covering my face in my hands, a terrifying thought struck me like a thunderbolt. My heart leapt in my throat. I understood the meaning of the image.

My mum's going to be boarding that plane. She's in danger!'
I gasped …

'Aurora, Wolfie!' I dashed up the beach yelling.

Aurora turned startled eyes on me. 'Calm down,
Lia! Tell me what's happened?'

'It's Mum, Aurora.' I choked the words out. She's in
terrible danger. Her plane's going to crash! It's true. I saw it
in a vision!'

She stared at me, horrified. 'Where did you see this?'

'Aurora, the vision was shown to me in the fire's
embers just now on the beach. Please believe me.'

Her face drained. 'I do believe you. She grasped my
shoulder. 'We have to return home immediately Lia. There's
no time to lose.' She wrung her hands in agitation, 'there is
work to be done. This time we must finish it!'

My scalp prickled. 'What do you mean?'

She levelled solemn eyes at mine. 'The vision you
had was a warning from Tyra to us Lia. She has not been
defeated and is still intent on doing us great harm.'

My stomach clenched. 'You mean she's still a threat?'

'I mean she has not been vanquished and is hell-
bent on destroying us.' She blinked rapidly, 'and unless we
do something now she may well succeed. I'm afraid for
your mother.'

'We have to do something now!'

Chapter 26

Aurora gave the broomstick strict instructions and it flew like the wind getting us home in what seemed to me like a mere blink of an eye.

She sat herself down at her kitchen table and began to write a list.

'Now let me see.' She perched her glasses on the end of her nose. 'I'm sure I have most of the items I need but you will have to go out to gather these.' She handed me her list repeating, 'A bunch of red Clover for luck, and white for breaking curses, and a Foxglove to lure, oh and a few twigs from the Rowan tree to protect us.' I nodded and set off to collect them immediately.

Having found everything she had asked for I burst into her kitchen calling out, 'Aurora. I've brought back everything on your list.'

'That's grand, dearie.' She looked up; her face flushed from stooping over heat radiating out from her big black cauldron. Stirring the bubbling, steaming brew, she muttered. 'Please don't interrupt me, Lia. I'm at a crucial point in my spell-making.'

'What are you brewing?' I asked.

'Shhhush!' She drew her brows together, adding something yellow to the cauldron.

The kitchen's chaotic state told me there had been a flurry of activity. Various-sized bottles of jewel-coloured liquids were set out on her table. Alongside them were plants, crystals, candles and a witch's stone knife. I sneaked a look at the spell book lying open at Chapter 17 and read,

Transformations:
Subheadings –
Metamorphosis, Transmutation, Mutation, Transmogrification, Shapeshifting.

'Can I help?' I offered, placing my basket of plants down in front of her.

Wiping her hands on her apron, she pushed her stray hair back from her face and gave me a strange look.

'Aye, I will need your help, bairn, but first we should talk. There now. That can sit for a minute.' She lifted the heavy cauldron from the heat and set it down on the flagstones. 'Let's sit a piece.' Collapsing into a seat at the table, she fanned herself with her apron. 'Phew, ma heid's fair burstin'.' She closed her eyes for a moment then spoke in a low-pitched voice. 'Come and sit by me, Lia.' She patted the chair next to her.

'What is it? What's wrong, Aurora?'

She placed her hand over mine. 'Lia. I'm going to ask something very difficult of you. You see I can't defeat Tyra on my own. I need your help.

'What can I do?' I said in a small voice my stomach

207

flipping over.

Aurora rubbed her forehead. 'I've been giving it a deal o' thought. If we challenged her to a battle, we may not win. She will summon all her forces to fight for her. We have to outwit her.'

All my senses became alert. 'But how will we do that?'

She squeezed my hand. 'You still have much to learn in the art of sorcery, Lia, but I have a plan. I'm going to ask you to be very brave, can you do that?' Her grave look told me she had something difficult and dangerous in mind.

I thought of Tyra's threat to put my mother in danger and knew she had to be stopped. I had no option but to agree. Coming to a quick decision I blurted, 'What do you want me to do?'

'Did you know magic runs on energy, Lia? Tyra has weakened her magic by channelling too much of her energy into destructive deeds. She is close to burning herself out and is desperate to replenish her vigour by stealing yours. You must seek her out. You must make yourself a target for her wrath. You have to enrage her to such an extent that she uses up the last of her magical reserves in an attempt to obliterate you. I can't do this myself. I am too old. You are young. Your magic is potent. You have the strength to do this, and I can help you.'

I suppressed a shiver and nodding my head I agreed. 'I'll do what you ask of me, but where will I find her?'

'Ah!' Aurora lifted her hands. 'That's no' a problem. Just as she always knows where I am, I know her whereabouts. She's crawled back to her underground lair in the caves where she believes darkness gives her protection.'

I flinched. 'The caves. Don't say I have to go back there?'

She patted my hand. 'Don't worry. You will not go in your current form. I am preparing a spell of transmogrification.'

'I know what transmogrification means!' I gaped at her. 'I'm to be turned into something!'

'Yes!' She nodded vigorously. 'You will be transformed into a bat.'

'A bat!' I gawped at her.

'Of course a bat,' she stressed. 'It's the perfect cover. Bats have excellent night vision. They're also difficult to spot in the dark. It will allow you to get close to her, and once you are within her presence you will reveal yourself. You will take her by surprise. In her rage, she will vent her fury, and in her violent anger she will lose control of the last of her power. The best way to weaken a witch is to keep her from her element. Tyra's element is earth and water. She cannot tolerate fire. You will lure her out from her underground lair where I will be ready.'

Shaking my head, my voice wavering, I said, 'I'm afraid.'

'I know, child, but you have to trust me. In my spell

of transmogrification, I will build in a protective shield to surround you so completely that Tyra's sorcery cannot penetrate or reach you. She will not harm you.' Aurora stared into my eyes. 'I would never put you into any danger. You are far too precious to me.'

I exhaled a long breath. 'All right. I'll do it.'

She gave me a look. 'You are sure?'

'I'm sure.' I nodded.

She gripped the arm of the chair and pushed herself up. 'Then let's get started. Chop some of this for me, dear, would you?' She indicated the white clover. 'For breaking curses, and do add a handful of four-leaf clover for good luck and success.'

Adding the chopped greens to the cauldron mix she chanted her words:

What she has brought down on me
Be now returned, but as times three,
Head to toe, skin and nerves,
May she get what she deserves.

She turned to Wolfie, who sat bolt upright, eyes glued to her every move.

Wolf, with your wiles, your instinct,
and might,
lend us your wisdom and strength
this night.

Wolfie bowed his head to her.

'Then it's agreed,' Aurora concluded. 'We will travel by teleportation.' I heard a hint of anxiety in her voice.

'We? Are you coming with me?'

'I am. I will transform myself into the guise of a black crow which' – she held up a finger – 'will also signify a change for good.'

'Aurora, I don't mean to question your judgement, but are you sure your spell of teleportation won't go wrong this time? Wouldn't it be safer to travel on the broomstick?'

She shook her head. 'Too visible for this important mission.' We mustn't alert Tyra to our presence. She must not have time to prepare herself.'

Aurora pored over the spell book and, speaking in a brisk tone, said, 'I've checked and rechecked my ingredients. I've measured everything with great care. I'm quite confident there will be no mishaps.' Wolfie raised his eyes heavenward but said nothing. Aurora clapped her hands. 'As time is of the essence, will we make ready?'

She handed me a little sachet of a powdery mix that at first glance looked like ashes, and fixed serious eyes on mine. 'Handle it with extreme caution, Lia. It must be treated with the greatest respect. It contains a high element of dark magic and used in the wrong hands can be extremely dangerous.

I cupped it carefully in my palms and became aware of it glowing like red coal embers.

'This is a spell which has formidable consequences.' She held up a finger. 'You must guard it well and take great care to use it only when the time is right. 'She threaded the sachet onto a black cord and handed it to me.

Fighting rising panic, I tied it around my neck. 'But how will I know when the time is right? How can I be sure?'

'You have to trust your judgement. You will know.' She touched a finger to the sachet and closed her eyes tight, repeating her magic. Next Aurora sprinkled salt in a circle and bid me step inside – 'for protection,' she said.

'Drink this, Lia.' She handed me a phial of murky green-coloured elixir.

I gulped it down before I had time to change my mind. She and Wolfie drank the other two phials. Moments after I swallowed the potion a loud piercing noise echoed in my ears. Then everything went black.

Chapter 27

Wherever I'd pitched up felt cold and damp. I sniffed the musty air and peered into the darkness as blind as a bat. My heart lurched. Oh jeezzz … I am a bat!

I clung on by my claws seeing everything from an upside-down perspective – the floor of the cave appeared to be the roof. I wriggled myself free from whatever it was pressing in on me. Hardly daring to breathe I found myself hemmed in by a colony of bats. I wanted to scream but I could only manage a high-pitched squeak. I listened … Even the tiniest noise seemed intense bouncing off the walls of the cave and rebounding back at me. I discovered I had a kind of radar giving me signals and information about my surroundings. I eased myself out from the crush of bats, thankful they were frozen in a state of hibernation. Tentatively I spread out my wings and found I could fly. As I moved in a kind of breaststroke movement, it felt like swimming through the air. I searched the cave for a good hiding place and squeezed myself into a tight chink in the wall where I could sense what was around me but not be detected.

Suddenly I heard Aurora's voice in my head. 'Stay hidden and don't make a move until I tell you it's time. … If Tyra feels any shift in the magical equilibrium around her, she will sense a threat.'

Too late! A familiar dreadful stench made my blood run cold. A hideous creature covered in slimy green scales slithered and crawled along the cave floor below me. I shrank back as it raised its head, nostrils flaring, sniffing, so close I could sense its cruel yellow eyes seeking me out, its putrid breath disgusting me as it drew closer. Aurora communicated with me telepathically, her voice sounding shaky.

'Be careful, Lia! Tyra has transformed herself into one of the most deadliest monsters known to the mythological world – the Basilisk. Listen well to me. The beast's most lethal weapon is its deadly gaze. Confront the creature and lure it into the open. Draw it out, but do not under any circumstances meet its gaze. First its stare entrances you, then renders you powerless; finally it spits toxic venom. If you look into its eyes, it will kill you! Remember you must not …' Her voice faded.'

'Aurora, don't leave me?' I tried to reach out to her, but my connection to her had died.

$$\ast \; \ast \; \ast \; \ast \; \ast$$

Now there was only myself to rely on. To win I had to come out fighting! My heart pounded, waiting for my moment. Hearing the slimy beast rumble closer, I knew I had to act quickly. Bursting forth from my hiding place, I frantically beat my wings around its head, distracting it, luring it forward to the mouth of the cave. It roared in rage, snapping its great jaws while I darted in and out of its vision. Coming to rest on a wide ledge at the mouth of the cave, I believed myself safely out of its reach and chose this moment to morph back into myself.

Looking down on the monster I cried out, taunting it:

I am Vanilia Solveig, White Witch of the Wind the Sea and the House of Strength ...

'...I am here to settle a score with you, Tyra. Let this be our day of reckoning. You are a despicable, low creature. I have come to rid this world of your evil once and for all.'

The creature bellowed so hard plumes of black smoke came out of its nostrils, and with a savage roar it made an attempt to lunge at me.

I poured scorn over her. 'Do not underestimate me or believe for even one moment that I am afraid of you, Tyra. I hold you in the deepest contempt. You are but a miserable, feeble nothing, worthy only of my disdain!'

Erupting in fury, the beast sprang again. This time I took a desperate leap from the ledge and landed a few feet in front of the enraged beast. Fleeing from the cave, my terror mounted with every step, sensing it gaining on me, following just a hairbreadth behind. Determined to succeed, I clutched the precious powdered spell in my hand waiting until I felt its hot breath on the back of my neck, and just as it bore down on me I whirled around. Keeping my eyes tight closed, I blew the deadly powder full into the monster's face.

The magical powder blew up a sandstorm, creating a swirling curtain of red gritty mist. I heard the creature wail as it thrashed around, frustrated in its attempt to lay hold of me. Something alighted on my shoulder as I stumbled around, choking, suffocated by the blanket of swirling red dust. A shiny black crow blinked a beady eye at me, and a second later Aurora morphed into herself. She stood with me amid the storm and raising her arms she called out in a forceful voice:

Here and now I evoke
the elemental force of fire.
I call you forth so that I
might bring about change.
Fire, I call thee hence!

The dust settled, and we became encircled by a sea of flames. Intense, fierce heat melted the red sand into liquid, which began to mould itself into the shape of a black glass mirror.

'Don't be afraid, Lia.' Aurora sensed my terror. 'I call on the element of fire not to destroy but to bring about change. When it is powerful and pure enough, fire's strength can take the urges to dominate and destroy and transform them into the desire to heal and renew the world.'

She raised her palms. The fire died, and I saw through the haze of dust and smoke a poor pathetic ragged woman, tears streaming down her face, crouched like a whipped dog at Aurora's feet. Aurora looked down on her in pity. She raised her voice and called to the spirits.

'Let the healing process begin!' Leaning down, she helped the weeping woman to her feet. 'Look, Tyra,' Aurora implored her, 'the sand has melted and has turned into a looking-glass creating a soul mirror. Look deep into it and behold the dark chambers of your life. In this cleansing of fire let the dark forces leave you and the forces of good be again restored. Look at your reflection, Tyra. This mirror is a window into your dark soul. Behold the pain and destruction you've caused. If you can feel true remorse and seek forgiveness, you can bring about a transformation. You will again become the good and beloved sister you once were before you became lost to me so long ago.'

Aurora held Tyra's arm in a fierce grip, forcing her to look into the black silvered mirror:

Let her feel shame at what she has done,
And change her ways
before more harm's done.
Undo her pain, teach her this night,
to make her peace and do what's right.

Tyra kept her head bent, still weeping, refusing to look at her reflection.

Aurora begged her. 'Tyra, my sister, you weren't born wicked. You must permit light to shine into your soul. Feel shame and sorrow for your evil deeds and seek forgiveness.'

Tyra twisted away, snarling, 'I will not.'

Aurora let out a sigh and said, her voice cracking, 'Then I cannot save you.' She thrust Tyra away from her. Tyra gave a high-pitched wail as she crumpled to the ground in a heap. I stared in horror as, before my eyes, she disintegrated into a pile of red dust. A whisper of wind turned into a stiff breeze which picked up her ashes and scattered them to the four winds.

Once it was over and calm was restored, a grey streak barrelled towards us from the mouth of the cave.

Wolfie screeched to a halt at Aurora's feet and stood panting. She crouched down and threw her arms around him. 'Ah, Wolfie. I've missed you. Where were you?'

'Tyra bewitched me,' he panted. 'I got trapped in her labyrinth and couldn't find my way out.'

'It's no matter, Wolfie,' Aurora soothed.

'Will Mum fly home safely now Aurora?' I asked in an anxious voice.

'Yes Lia.' She replied squeezing my hand. 'Tyra can do no more harm now. Her time is over. We can all go home safely.'

Chapter 28

So much has happened in the last few months. I'm now attending the local school. My tuition in witchcraft with Aurora continues at weekends. Today, Saturday, I rose with the dawn and explored the hedgerows, foraging for plants and roots, collecting only the freshest of them for my lesson. I returned to Aurora's home feeling very pleased with myself and placed my full basket on her table, filling her kitchen with a heady aroma of mint and chamomile.

'Ah,' she said, lifting a sprig of mint to her nose and inhaling deeply. 'Did you know herbs and plants are at their most potent now in midsummer when the sun is at the height of its powers. That's a grand mixter-maxter you've gathered for us this morning. I'm going use this mint to make floor wash to invite happiness and good fortune into the house.'

'And look, Aurora. I found some chamomile.' I buried my nose in the fragrance of the delicate white and yellow daisy heads. 'What will we use it for?'

'I'll use it to make tea. Lovely soothing chamomile tea. I'm going to make myself a cup now to drink while I'm sitting listening to you play.'

For the past few months Aurora had been teaching me to play the fiddle.

'Beautiful, Lia,' Aurora praised after listening to me

play my piece of music. (I'd been practising it for weeks.)

'You're becoming a fine musician.'

'Thanks. I just hope I don't make any mistakes tomorrow night,' I said, laying my bow down on her kitchen table. 'Should I play it again?'

'Yes. Once more, please,' she said with a nod, 'and remember you must strive to feel the music rise from your soul.'

I drew my hand across the bow and the first feeling of the sound rose from my tapping foot and flowed all the way through me to my elbow. I loved playing the fiddle, the lilting notes making my heart lift.

The summer solstice celebrations took place every year on Orkney at the Ring of Brodgar. I felt a shiver of anticipation. I would be playing my fiddle tomorrow night in front of the whole community.

'Only one more day to practise! I can't wait! I'm so excited. I've never been up to the Standing Stones.

'Aye, weel, it is a special place.' Aurora looked up from chopping chamomile. 'Some say magic has fled the world,' – she waggled her finger – 'but we know it has taken refuge in the few places left it can thrive. The Ring of Brodgar is one such a place. Some call it the Temple of the Sun. There is a legend the ancient stones were huge lumbering giants. Bowed down, they trudge round in an unending circle.'

'How did they get there, Aurora?' I hoped she would pause to tell me the tale, and I sat down beside her, propping my chin in my palm.

'Weel, that is an interesting question.' She lifted her shoulders in a half-shrug. 'The answer is nobody knows. Some say a very long time ago a group of fearsome giants crossed the causeway onto the Ness of Brodgar. They heard a fiddler play a rousing reel. The giants joined hands and whooping and shouting began to dance. The ground beneath their feet began to tremble as the colossal dancers whirled round and round, faster and faster. They were so enjoying the dance they forgot to pay attention to how fast the night was passing. Before they knew it, the morning sun crept into the sky and touched them with its early rays, turning them into cold hard stone.' Her eyes twinkled 'And there they remain frozen, rigid in the circle in which they danced.'

'And what happened to the fiddler?' I piped up, curious.

She held up a finger. 'A short distance from the giants' stones stands a solitary stone – the remains of the fiddler.'

I felt a surge of excitement. 'Tell me about the summer solstice celebrations. What happens?'

She steepled her fingers and eyed me over the top of her specs. 'Weel, it stays light all through the night in midsummer so everyone will stay up very late. Bonfires will be lit. There'll be music and dancing and feasting on honey cakes and ale …'

'Yaaay,' I interrupted her, dancing around her kitchen while playing a lively jig on my fiddle.
'Hey, buddo, she laughed, 'drink some of this chamomile tea to calm yourself doon!'

The soft light was truly magical on midsummer's night. Mum drove us over to the West Mainland. We parked the car and walked through a wildflower meadow over land sloping down between two lochs, shaped to look like a natural caldron by the surrounding hills.

'Over there.' Aurora stepped in front of us, pointing into the distance to a blazing bonfire which had turned the sky above it fiery crimson. My excitement bubbled over as I followed after her.

It looked like the whole of the community had gathered to celebrate the summer solstice. As we came closer, my heart leapt in excitement as I heard the steady rhythm of pounding drums which drew us into the crowds. Youngsters delirious with delight capered and danced around the fire. The warm night had brought everyone out in a party mood. We wandered over to join them and when settled down, sitting on springy heather mounds I gazed up at the awesome ring of towering giant stones.

The party was in full swing. We shared out our food, drank, gossiped, joked and laughed.

A black cat appeared from nowhere and began to rub its face on my leg. When I put my hand down to stroke it, in a blink of an eye it morphed into Megan!

'Ha! Got you! Got you!' she said in a singsong voice, flopping down beside me.

'Megan!' I giggled. 'Where did you come from?' I hooked my arm into hers. We were laughing so hard we both fell backwards.

'I live here, goofy. Remember?' she answered in a teasing voice. 'I'm starting the same school as you in a couple of weeks. We're going to be classmates!'

'Yaaaay,' I shouted jubilantly.

The crowd gave me enthusiastic applause after I played my piece of music, 'The Fairy Dance,' a lively reel. Afterwards, people came up to me eager to show their appreciation. They made me feel I belonged, and their

223

kindness brought my mum's words back to me: 'They're a community of good kind people and accepting of those who are a wee bit different.'

Oystercatchers perching on the tops of the giant standing stones flew off into a dawn-streaked sky and people began to drift home.

'Time to go,' Mum said, packing up our things. She turned to Megan. 'Why don't you come round to our house tomorrow?'

'That'll be great!' Megan replied, 'though it's already tomorrow!'

'So it is, Megan.' Mum laughed. 'Well, go home for a sleep and you can come round to ours for supper later.' I nodded, 'Yeah, come round and we can conjure up some frosted crescent moon cakes.'

A light breeze stirred as Mum and I walked down the sandy path to our cottage.

'I'm still buzzing from playing my fiddle in front of all those people. It was great meeting up with Megan, Mum. Thanks for asking her round. She's really nice. You'll like her.'

'I already do.' She smiled. 'I think you two will be best friends.'

'I'll never get to sleep, Mum. I'm far too wide awake. I'm going to sit out a while. I want to watch the sun come up.'

'OK, darlin'.' She draped her jacket around my shoulders. 'I'm going in. Don't let yourself get cold.'

I took my fiddle down to the beach and sat on my favourite rock looking out over the calm bay. The sun came up over the horizon bathing me in a rosy glow. It rose over the ocean creating a magical mosaic of reflected colours. I took up my fiddle and drew my bow back and forth playing a haunting lament, 'The Song of the Brave Fisherman.'

I played it slow, the music harmonising with the murmur of the ebbing tide.

The waves softly dousing the sand had a hypnotic effect. As I gazed out across the horizon, the sound of another fiddle drifted across the water to me. I caught sight of the hazy outline of a figure standing on the shoreline between high and low water. As my eyes adjusted, I saw he was a tall, strong, redheaded man draped in a silver seal skin. He stood absolutely still, captured in a shaft of sunshine, and turning striking green eyes on me he played a tune which will always be special to me, 'The Sea Maid'. I listened mesmerised, and when he finished playing the piece, he raised his hand in salute to me before vanishing into the shimmering sea-haze.

I knew then with absolute certainty that man was my father.

Sometimes we are lucky enough to know that our lives have been changed for the better. We can discard the old and embrace the new. It happened to me that midsummer.

Walking back up the beach towards the cottage, I couldn't think of a time I'd felt happier. With a sudden flare of joy, I shouted out at the top of my voice:

I am Vanilia Solveig, White Witch, born of the Wind, the Sea, and the House of Strength.

The End
- or is it (just the beginning)?

Joan Dewar

Joan Dewar is a FABULIST. Did that word raise your eyebrows? What on earth's a fabulist you ask? Does it mean she's fabulous? Well no it doesn't (although she is of-course.) F-A-B-U-L-I-S-T means FIBBER. Joan is a fibber, but not in a bad way. She just enjoys making up stories. Magical, fantastical, exceedingly greatical, right-up your-streetical stories, and sometimes, as she well knows after writing down an idea for a story, you can get lost and find a better one, an even bigger one, and you keep writing, and then you end up with a whole bloomin' book. Awesome!

Joan a full-time writer, lives in Edinburgh with her husband and her wee Border Terrier dog Geordie. She enjoys reading, creative writing, retrieving a ball for her lazy dog, eating Haribo star-mix, and travelling to 'otherworlds' both real and imaginary. Set off now on an adventure to say hi to her online at:

Web Site :www.joandewar.com

Face Book: https://fb.meJoanDewarAuthor

Twitter: @JoanDewarAuthor